RESCUE ME

What Reviewers Say About Julie Cannon's Work

Breaker's Passion is…"an exceptionally hot romance in an exceptionally romantic setting. …Cannon has become known for her well-drawn characters and well-written love scenes."—*Just About Write*

In *Power Play*…"Cannon gives her readers a high stakes game full of passion, humor, and incredible sex."—*Just About Write*

About *Heartland*…"There's nothing coy about the passion of these unalike dykes—it ignites at first encounter and never abates. … Cannon's well-constructed novel conveys more complexity of character and less overwrought melodrama than most stories in the crowded genre of lesbian-love-against-all-odds—a definite plus." —Richard Labonte, *Book Marks*

"Cannon has given her readers a novel rich in plot and rich in character development. Her vivid scenes touch our imaginations as her hot sex scenes touch us in many other areas. *Uncharted Passage* is a great read."—*Just About Write*

About *Just Business*…"Julie Cannon's novels just keep getting better and better! This is a delightful tale that completely engages the reader. It's a must read romance!"—*Just About Write*

Visit us at www.boldstrokesbooks.com

By the Author

Come and Get Me

Heart 2 Heart

Heartland

Uncharted Passage

Just Business

Power Play

Descent

Breaker's Passion

Rescue Me

RESCUE ME

by
Julie Cannon

2011

RESCUE ME
© 2011 By Julie Cannon. All Rights Reserved.

ISBN 10: 1-60282-582-3
ISBN 13: 978-1-60282-582-6

This Trade Paperback Original Is Published By
Bold Strokes Books, Inc.
P.O. Box 249
Valley Falls, NY 12185

First Edition: December 2011

Credits
Editor: Shelley Thrasher
Production Design: Susan Ramundo
Cover Design By Sheri (graphicartist2020@hotmail.com)

Acknowledgments

This book was the toughest one for me to complete. I took a new job, moved my family halfway across the country, and worked eighty-hour weeks for months under incredible pressure. Throw in a new puppy and a new school for the kids, and there wasn't much time for anything else. But then again my life isn't that much different from anyone else's. I'm very fortunate to have a family that is always there even when I'm not quite there to encourage me to keep at it. Thanks to Rad for giving me the extra time I needed, for Shelley for always knowing the right words, Sheri for transferring the image in my head to the cover, and everyone else who makes our work come to life for our readers.

Enjoy!

Dedication

To Laura:
Just because and always

CHAPTER ONE

"You want me to do what?"

"Come on, Tyler. It's not that bad."

"That's a matter of opinion," Tyler replied, her fingers dancing over the almost-soundless keyboard.

"When was the last time I asked you for anything?"

"Last week."

"Okay. Well, when was the last time I asked you for something like this?"

Tyler stopped typing and looked at the phone on her desk as if she could see Paul through the speaker at the end of the line. Even though he was her best friend and was right, she still didn't want to do this. It was absurd. "There is no way I'm going to sit around with a bunch of straight people and pretend to be your girlfriend for five days. I've done it before, Paul, at a cocktail party or a fancy dinner with a client. But five days is four days and twenty hours too long."

"Tyler." Paul's voice turned serious. "You know how much this means to me. I wouldn't ask if I really didn't need you."

"Paul, when are you going to man-up and come out of your office closet? You've made that company millions. If they don't like it tell them to get fucked."

"It's not that simple, Tyler, and you know it. I don't have more money than God and men and women following my every word, like you do. I've told you, I need one more big deal in my pocket before I can write my own ticket and get any job I want. Do you think I like it? Give me some credit. This is a means to an end, nothing more. Come on, Tyler, please." His voice was almost a whine, which set her teeth on edge.

Tyler tiptoed around her real hesitation about going on this trip. "Paul, you know I can't do this."

"Says who?"

"Paul…" Tyler began trying to find the words that normally came easily.

"Tyler, you can't not do things because you're afraid."

"I'm not afraid." Get a grip, Tyler thought, after she realized she'd practically shouted into the phone.

"Yes, Tyler, you are. Look at your life, your relationships with women. You've buried yourself in your books, behind Blake, and you haven't been out on a real date in I don't know how long."

"Who died and made you my date monitor?"

"I'm your best friend, Tyler. That and a myriad of other duties make up that job description. Now, am I right or am I right?"

Paul was nothing but always brutally honest with her, and most times she loved him for it. But this was another matter altogether. *Normal* definitely had a new meaning. He wasn't living in her shoes. He didn't wake up in the morning and see what she saw every day. An empty bed and… He didn't give her a chance to answer.

"Come on, Tyler." His voice softened like it always did when he showed her how much he cared for her. "Do it for me. No, do it for you." Paul corrected himself emphatically. He continued his sales pitch, which, unbeknownst to him, wasn't necessary. "They have electricity, indoor plumbing, and a satellite phone. It's not like we'll be living like the Swiss Family Robinson. I've seen pictures of the house. It's fabulous."

He would know, Tyler thought. Paul had a natural decorating flair he kept hidden from his tight-ass boss and equally homophobic colleagues. But he had turned it loose on her house and she would be forever grateful. The only thing she knew about decorating was writing the check.

Tyler recognized his comment for what it was. He was trying to take the serious edge off the turn the conversation had taken. He was trying to get her to laugh. At times he was the only one who could, and because of that she said, "All right, but you owe me big time. And I mean B-I-G time."

"You won't be disappointed. I promise you'll enjoy yourself. I'll make sure of it. You won't regret this."

Tyler hung up but not before murmuring, "Yeah, right." Somehow she knew better.

CHAPTER TWO

Kristin Walker hated these business functions. Entertaining the wives, the mindless small talk, idiotic chatter about the weather, and the latest crisis involving the spoiled children of her husband's employees were enough to make her head pop. More than once she wanted to tell these pampered women that their children needed a swat on the butt once in a while and limits—not those associated with a Platinum American Express card.

Most of all she hated being on display. She was the boss's wife and, with her position, came the stifling requirements to constantly be the pillar of decorum, good taste, and the latest fashion. She really wanted to stay home in her favorite old T-shirt she kept hidden in the bottom drawer of her dresser, dunk Oreos in milk, and watch old sci-fi B movies. At least she'd set the Ti-Vo to record the Mars-invasion marathon scheduled to run the week they'd be out of town.

She was bored. After the incident, Steven refused to let her work. He masked his decision by telling people that even with an MBA from the Sloan School of Business, she preferred being a stay-at-home wife who supported him behind the scenes. She couldn't conceive of a statement further from the truth. He told her in private that no wife of his was going to work, even though she suspected it was more than that. He didn't want her around, even if it was her family's business. Or at least it used to be. But where she found herself now was her doing, and hers alone. She never regretted her decision but often wished it hadn't come with so many strings. Kristin could swear they were tightening around her neck.

Kristin looked at the neatly packed suitcase while she mentally ticked off the agenda on the ridiculous event next week. Three of Steven's employees and their spouses would meet Monday morning at the hangar where Steven parked his plane and they'd fly to the island. That was almost correct. Two of the three had a spouse. Paul, her husband's chief of strategy, was the only single one in the bunch, even though Tyler often accompanied him to spouse-required business events.

She thought about "Paul's Tyler." When she first met Tyler at the company Christmas party several years ago, she had expected something quite different from the tall, regal, self-confident woman who walked into the restaurant with Paul. Her hair was dark, almost black, and shockingly short yet not at all masculine. She wore an exquisite Vera Wang suit in a beautiful shade of deep plum. Kristin couldn't keep her eyes off her as they headed directly toward her and Steven. Tyler had a slight limp but didn't hesitate when Paul introduced her and she shook Steven's hand.

When she repeated the greeting and thanked Kristin for the invitation, Kristin's breath hitched when Tyler looked at her. Her eyes were pale blue, unusual for a woman with otherwise dark features, and were cautious when she gazed at Kristin. Her voice was smooth and melodic, reminding Kristin of good scotch whiskey. When their hands touched, Tyler's was warm and softer than Kristin anticipated. Something about her was familiar in an oddly comfortable way. Kristin didn't warm up to people easily, especially those related to Steven's job. She had to keep her guard up at all times when most of the time she wanted to sit by the pool, her feet up, drinking a Hurricane.

She Googled Tyler Logan the next morning and, fascinated, read every article about her. Tyler, a critically acclaimed author of a series of action/adventure novels, had, according to *Publishers Weekly*, "millions of fans around the world anxiously awaiting her latest release, *Expedition*, the next book in a series featuring Blake Hudson." Kristin had read every Tyler Logan book twice and easily admitted to herself and no one else that she was one of those eager fans.

Three years and more functions than she cared to count had passed, and she found herself looking forward to seeing Tyler each time. Regardless of the circumstances, whether it be a dinner party or Christmas celebration, she always kept one eye on the door until Tyler and Paul arrived.

"Mrs. Walker, the caterer is here."

The housekeeper Steven insisted on employing spoke quietly from behind her. They didn't need her, but she had lost that argument and so many others with Steven she no longer even tried. What was the point? He'd overwhelm her with words like *status, entitled*, their position in the community, his reputation, blah, blah, blah. She didn't care about all that. Never did, never would. Certainly not now. She had never been interested in keeping up with the Joneses, and now that she was the Joneses, the achievement wasn't what everyone thought it was cracked up to be.

"Thank you, I'll be right down," she said to the hovering servant she knew had a direct line to Steven. On more than one occasion Steven had information about what she had done or worn that could only have come from her. After all, the woman knew who signed her paychecks. With a sigh, she turned and headed downstairs.

❖

"Are you planning to wear that thing on your ear all night?" Paul asked as he turned onto the street where his boss's house dominated the cul-de-sac.

Tyler waved him off as she continued her conversation. "I'm sorry, Roberta, but I told you several times in the last week I'll be out of town. You'll have to handle this on your own or it'll have to wait until I get back." She listened for a few seconds. "No, I won't be reachable by phone. I'll be on some godforsaken island in the middle of nowhere. This is why I hired you. This is your job, not mine." Tyler had had this same conversation with Roberta two days earlier. Getting nowhere, she said her good-byes and hung up.

Tyler had landed in Houston late that afternoon in time to get to Paul's house, shower, change, and get to this pre-trip dinner. The week had been a blur as she worked to get everything settled at home, enabling herself to go on this ridiculous trip. And to top it off her flight arrived late, typical for practically every departure from San Francisco lately.

She was tired, having not slept much the night before, preferring to venture out to her favorite club—the one with no name and a very discreet clientele. It had been several weeks since she'd visited it and she was getting antsy. Between this trip and other commitments, it would be at least another three before she'd have any time to venture out, so she made time even if it cost her several hours of desperately needed sleep.

Venture out. What an odd way to phrase what she did. It was almost clinical, definitely sterile, and just the way she needed it. The club was in an old warehouse whose exterior verified its age, but inside it was all chrome, glass, and glamour. She paid a hefty price to remain on the guest list and never regretted it. And last night had been no exception.

The soundproofing of the building was perfection. Absolutely no sound emanated from the brick building she had stood outside. Several times while waiting to be admitted, Tyler swore she heard crickets chirping. But once inside, everything changed.

She stepped through a series of mantraps, small individual rooms with four walls, a ceiling, and a door opposite the one she stepped through. This elaborate architecture kept the private club, well, private, and the noise from leaking into the street. She had learned of the club from a friend who had died from cancer and left her membership to Tyler. It was more than odd and Tyler was more than confused when the attorney contacted her to give her the information.

After months she finally ventured into the club, following the bizarre set of instructions in the sealed white envelope the attorney had given her three years earlier. Knock five times, count to three, then knock again. Secret words and a small blue-and-white card got her through the final gauntlet. Once inside and a few drinks later she promised she would never, ever venture into any other lesbian bar.

Last night the woman had been a redhead, or at least Tyler thought she was. Tyler had spotted her a few minutes after she arrived, and it wasn't long before they were in one of the private rooms she paid extra for. The lights were intentionally low, providing a sense of anonymity for the guests. Tyler considered it a false sense of security because how anonymous can you be when someone's face is inches from yours? She didn't go for the masks like some of the others, but to each her own, she often said. Tyler didn't know why the others were there. Whether having sex with complete strangers turned them on, or they too had something to hide, it didn't matter to Tyler. She didn't have to make small talk, pretend it was something other than sex she wanted, and never had to completely expose herself.

The lock barely clicked when the woman's lips were on hers, anxious hands tugging at her shirt. As was Tyler's usual modus operandi, she had the woman pinned against the door, naked and gasping for breath, in less than five minutes. Tyler was completely clothed; however, her belt was open, her zipper down.

Tyler was much taller than the redhead, which made it handy, so to speak, for the woman to straddle Tyler's thigh. Tyler didn't care about the telltale traces of desire on her pants. She focused on only one thing—the woman in her arms.

They exchanged kisses, each fighting for dominance, each relinquishing control. Lips ravaged, tongues mated, and teeth bit. Tyler kept the woman's hands above her head, giving her free rein to explore the luscious curves and intoxicating scent of the woman. She didn't bother with light, soft caresses; the woman didn't want them and that wasn't what they were there for. Nibbles and teasing licks were for lovers; this was fast, furious, and completely basic. In other words, raw sex.

Tyler bit on one nipple while her hand explored farther south. The woman eagerly spread her legs, giving Tyler silent permission to take whatever she wanted. Tyler did, boldly plunging inside the woman.

Her fingers easily slid in and out, the stranger's juices coating Tyler's hand. She flicked her clit back and forth with her thumb, and before long the woman muffled her scream by sinking her teeth into Tyler's shoulder as she came.

Tyler's arousal had climbed along with the woman's and she was aching for release. She shifted slightly and the woman quickly returned the favor, her hands mimicking what Tyler's had just completed. Stroke after stroke Tyler waited for the explosion that would release the pressure that had been building inside her. It was taking her longer to come this time, much longer than the last and the time before that. What used to take minutes now took practically forever, and if she didn't completely concentrate she might not come at all. She waited and waited, and when she finally felt the familiar tingling in the pit of her stomach she focused on imagining the rush of orgasm spreading through her body.

It was over almost before she knew it. Her orgasms were far less powerful and cataclysmic than before as well. Maybe her age caused the difference. She was thirty-nine and had read that as a woman ages, her orgasms change. Once, just once, for a fleeting moment Tyler thought that maybe she should blame the fact that her climax satisfied her body but did nothing for her soul. She quickly banished that thought.

Tyler hung up as Paul stopped in front of his boss's house. Every time she saw the monstrosity, she thought this was by far the ugliest house she had ever seen. It was modern, sleek construction, a maze of sharp angles and chrome that she swore would someday come to life and fly into space. It was the perfect image of its owner and what she secretly hoped would happen to him.

She had despised Steven Walker from the moment she met him. Actually, even before she met him. If he was the type of boss that would fire her best friend just because he was gay, then she wanted nothing to do with him. But because Paul was her best friend she tolerated Steven and his pompous, blustering, self-righteous bullshit. She was sure tonight would not be any different. She needed to have her head examined to go on a weeklong retreat with him. Maybe she and Paul could pretend they were starved for each other and everyone would leave them alone. Yeah, another dream. Steven would probably like to watch.

Paul opened the passenger-side door of his BMW, extending his hand to help her out of the low-slung vehicle. This simple act and hundreds of other reasons were why Tyler would do anything for him.

They had met twenty years ago in high school when Tyler was the new kid and fell victim to the typical cruelties of teenagers who thought they were perfect and better than everybody else. She was overweight, wore thick glasses, had hair as limp as a mop and a chest as flat as her ten-year-old brother's. Paul, on the other hand, had thick blond hair, crystal-blue eyes, a perfect complexion, and was a shoo-in for homecoming king. He had been well over six feet in the tenth grade and at thirty-eight had grown into a strapping man that she often described as tall, dark, and Harlequin gorgeous. What Tyler knew, that no one else in the school even suspected, was that Paul Campbell was gay. Or, as Paul's father often phrased it, "as queer as a three-dollar bill."

Branch Oak, Arkansas was not a metropolis in anyone's imagination, and they had supported each other while Paul faked his way through dating, Tyler's first-kiss-turned-first-slap, and everything since. When Paul went to Purdue and Tyler to work at Walmart, they continued their friendship and somehow had grown closer. When her second book hit the bestseller list, Paul convinced her to go back to school and get her degree. He was the first person she hugged when she walked off the stage, thirty-three years old, a crisp diploma in hand. And then came the accident, when Paul really showed his true colors. She never would have made it through without him.

"You're the one who invited me on this trip. The least you can do is shut up long enough for me to get my shit together enough to be your adoring squeeze." Tyler loved their playful banter.

"You'll love it and you know it. Nothing to do but lie on the beach and—"

"Be bored shitless. Do I look like the kind of girl who enjoys doing nothing? The last time I did nothing I was in the womb." Her mother always said she came out moving and never stopped.

"You're a woman, Tyler. Fake it."

She jabbed at him and missed when the front door opened.

The housekeeper who had answered the door the half-dozen other times Tyler had been to this house greeted them and led them to the living room. On the way Tyler noticed that the flowers typically in place on the side table had been replaced by a large brass statue of an eagle scooping up a rabbit in its talons. It was so garish and distasteful. Tyler shuddered

A choir of loud voices reached her as they approached the living room. She recognized the harsh New York accent of Mark Starfield, the chief financial officer of PPH Development. By far the stuffiest, most conservative financial guy Tyler had ever met, he proudly displayed his wife Patty like a trophy, a role she was obviously born to play.

Tyler took a deep breath and slipped her arm through Paul's. "Here we go, sweetheart," she said under her breath.

CHAPTER THREE

The first person Tyler saw when she entered the room was Kristin Walker. Maybe because she was closest to the door, or maybe because she was their hostess and was supposed to greet them. Tyler certainly didn't instinctively look for her every time she attended one of these events. She always felt a little zing when she thought about Kristin Walker, something she attributed to a completely normal instinctive reaction to a beautiful woman. Other than helping Paul out, seeing Kristin was the only thing she looked forward to when they played their charade.

Kristin was stunning with her natural beauty that other women paid dearly for, yet would never be able to buy. Tyler suspected she was around her age, if not a few years younger. She was absolutely beautiful and tonight was no exception. Kristin was always perfectly dressed in the latest designer outfit and sparkling accessories, yet she never appeared to be pretentious or stuck up like the other wives. Her blue dress practically floated around her as she approached. She looked a little stressed around the edges but who didn't these days? Tyler had never seen her with her hair down and was stunned when she realized she wanted to touch the blond locks and see if they were as silky as they looked.

Kristin's smile filled her face and her eyes sparkled. She held out her hand. "Paul, good to see you again, and Tyler, I'm so glad you'll be joining us this week."

Paul spoke first, giving Tyler the chance to start breathing again. What the hell was going on? She hadn't reacted this way to Kristin before because she was her best friend's boss's wife and was definitely straight and unquestionably off-limits. Her visceral response now was an unexpected first. Paul nudged her out of her shocked stupor. "Thank you for inviting me, Kristin," she said, taking the small hand offered. Hers was much larger than their hostess's, and Tyler wanted to pull her close and kiss her. She shook off that image and smiled instead.

"Of course you're invited. This retreat is a reward for all the hard work Paul did on the merger and a treat for the significant others who were alone so much because of it. I know very well how many evenings I spent alone and can just imagine how difficult it was for everyone else as well."

Tyler realized she was still holding Kristin's hand and didn't want to let it go. Instead, she quickly released it.

"I know how much Paul loves his job. He was good, though, he called almost every night." It wasn't the exact truth but not an outright lie. She and Paul found it easier to stay as close to the truth as possible when discussing their "life together." Before she had a chance to add anything else, Steven slid away from the group he was talking to and headed their way. He waddled, a condition caused by the extra hundred pounds he carried around his middle. Tyler noticed his hair was much thinner than the last time she saw him, and the fact that his part was just above his left ear indicated he wasn't accepting it well.

"Paul, glad you could make it."

Like he had any choice, Tyler thought, pulling herself together. She had to be on her toes around Steven. He never offered his hand to her in polite greeting but she always did just to enjoy his reaction. He always hesitated and looked at it as if he might catch something if he touched her.

She braced for his greeting, which was always one step shy of being outright rude, at least she thought so. But she bit her tongue and tolerated it.

"And Tyler, still living in sin city and writing those books?" The tone of his voice was borderline condescending. She had no idea why he thought San Francisco was sin city. That moniker typically referred to Las Vegas. And because he was a chauvinistic asshole he obviously considered her literary success a fluke, if he even thought of it at all. She felt Paul stiffen next to her and tightened her hold on his arm, silently telegraphing to let it die.

"Something like that, yes, Steven." She gritted her teeth and smiled. As usual he looked from her face, to her hand, then back at her face before shaking it. His grip was lukewarm at best, his palm clammy. "Thank you for inviting us to the retreat. Paul can't say enough about it." That part was true. He couldn't say enough to convince her this was a good idea. He'd had to pull out the guilt trip to get her to agree.

"Well, all the spouses are invited, and if Paul here would ever pop the question you'd take your rightful place beside him as well."

Tyler knew what he really meant was that her place was behind him and under him, supporting him like a good little wife at home with a hot meal on the table every night at six.

"How do you know he hasn't?" Tyler couldn't help but ask.

He chuckled. "Because you'd be married. What woman could resist such an opportunity?"

Tyler glanced at Kristin before answering. She wore that deer-in-the-headlights look she often had when around her husband. Tyler felt a twinge of something for whatever the cause.

"Well, I'm not like most women, and I'm sure when both Paul and I are ready to get married, we will." But not to each other, she said to herself. She grabbed a glass of wine from a passing waiter. If this evening was anything like others, the drink wouldn't be her last.

The announcement that dinner was ready saved her from any other inane conversation. Name cards stood in front of every immaculate place setting, and one quick glance told Tyler that, with the exception of Kristin and Steven seated at each end of the expansive table, they were sitting boy, girl, boy, girl. It reminded her of first grade when Miss Stepp separated the girls from the boys to keep them from talking too much. Recalling other dinner parties with this same group, Tyler noted that some things never change.

Kristin sat at the end of the expansive table flanked by Robert Brown, a.k.a. Perry Mason. Robert looked exactly like the 1960s TV icon, including his black suit and skinny dark tie, and more than once Tyler had almost addressed him as such. He parted his dark, slightly wavy hair on the left with razor straightness, the dark rings under his eyes appearing more inherited than caused by sleepless nights.

Mark was to Kristin's left, then Robert's wife Joan. Mark, an imposing man standing almost seven feet tall, was the complete opposite of Robert. Whereas dark hair covered the tops of Robert's hands and peeked out from the cuff of his shirt, Mark had absolutely no hair on his head or anywhere Tyler could see. His bald white head reflected the light from the chandelier overhead, and she didn't even want to think if he was hairless anywhere else. Steven was flanked by Paul on his right and Patty, Mark's wife, on his left, who also sat next to Tyler.

Steven presided at the head of the table, and, unlike Jesus and his disciples, he looked like he was ruling over his kingdom. In absolute contrast, Kristin graced the other end. Tyler caught Paul's eye when they were seated. They signaled each other silently that this dinner would be as entertaining as usual.

Kristin wasn't directly in her line of sight, but Tyler could see her well enough in her peripheral vision. Heat flushed through her body. What in the hell was going on? She had no business reacting like this, certainly not with Kristin. Talk about playing with fire.

While Steven talked about the specifics of the trip that would begin the day after tomorrow, Tyler kept one ear tuned to Kristin's conversation. The men talked shop, politics, and the stock market while the women talked about the declining quality of clothes at Nordstrom's and the difficulty of finding "good help," obviously referring to the multitude of workers employed to do everything for them from cutting the grass to cleaning the toilet. She was busier than all these women put together, and she didn't have a housecleaner. She even changed the oil in her car.

On more than one occasion, Tyler noticed that Kristin never really agreed with the women or added anything substantial, but simply kept the conversation moving. That was a skill in and of itself—keeping your mouth shut. She, on the other hand, had yet to master that. She said what was on her mind and rarely pulled any punches, except in these situations. She wouldn't do anything to jeopardize Paul's career.

Dinner finally over, the men gathered in the study to smoke stinky cigars and other God-only-knew-what manly things, the women settling in the living room. Tyler didn't care for either place, instead dividing her time between both. At least until her brain was about to explode. God, she hated Paul for putting her in these situations. She didn't really hate him. She never could, but he sure made her life difficult at times.

She glanced around the room at the women practically holding court with Kristin. Talk about sucking up to the boss's wife. Joan, Robert's wife, had a stick so far up her butt Tyler was surprised it wasn't poking out the top of her head. She was pulled so tight, you could bounce a quarter off her face, and Tyler wondered how many shots of Botox it took to achieve that look. Her hair was dyed what Paul had once described as red number twelve, and the style mimicked that of the hottest actress on the big screen. It must take forever to get it to look like that, she thought. Patty Starfield, a complete airhead, giggled so often, Tyler almost did something she might regret.

Tyler had to spend a week with these chatty, mindless women?

She heard her name and realized with a start that Kristin had asked her a question. "I'm sorry, what did you say?" She was embarrassed to be caught not paying attention. Was that a smile of understanding on Kristin's face?

"I asked when Blake plans to have her next adventure."

"March," Tyler answered automatically, trying not to focus on the way Kristin's lips moved when she talked.

"Where do you get your ideas?" asked Patty, who again solidified Tyler's opinion of her. She asked that same question practically every time they were together. She was from Boston and the word *your* sounded more like *yaw*.

Tyler repeated the answer she always gave when asked, but this time, before one of the other women had a chance to change the subject, Kristin asked a follow-up question.

"How does Blake know about all the different survival techniques she uses?" Occasionally Kristin had asked questions about her writing, but only on the rare instances they were alone. The professional side of Tyler warmed when Kristin mentioned her main character by name. Every author strived to make her characters come to life. Blake was real to Kristin, and Kristin was suddenly very real to Tyler.

Tyler ignored the polite, bored looks on the other women's faces and focused on Kristin instead. "Do you remember a show on TV in the mid-eighties called *MacGyver*?"

"I've seen it on one of the old cable channels. I loved that show," Kristin replied, the first demonstration of genuine interest in a subject that Tyler could recall.

"I did too. I always wondered how they figured out all those things MacGyver did to get out of the situations he was in. When I first started writing, I bought all the old episodes I could get my hands on and watched them dozens of times. When I ran out of ideas I contacted the writers of the show and asked. One of them connected me with their technical staff and it just went from there." That sure sounded a lot easier than it actually was, she thought. But wasn't that the point of fiction?

"I always dreamed of traveling to exotic places like Blake does." Kristin stopped, a look of near-horror on her face at her answer.

"What happened?" Tyler prompted her, knowing by Kristin's expression that she wouldn't get an answer. She was wrong.

"Life." A flash of sadness passed over her face before the hostess mask fell firmly back into place.

Tyler's stomach did a little flip-flop and she had to focus, even though she knew better. She kept an eye on Kristin for the remaining conversation, but Kristin never made eye contact until they were saying their good-byes at the front door. Tyler spoke first and held out her hand .

"Thank you again for dinner and the conversation, Kristin." Finally Kristin looked at her, this time with something in her eyes other than politeness, but Tyler wasn't sure what it was. Kristin's hand was cool but warmed an instant after Tyler took it. This time when she held it Tyler put her left hand over Kristin's and held it there for a second. Fright flashed in Kristin's green eyes and Tyler immediately let go, afraid she had overstepped. She turned her attention to Steven and repeated her thanks before Paul took her arm and escorted her out the door.

❖

"I'm glad that's over," Tyler said, slipping off her shoes. "How do you put up with those people?" She didn't expect Paul to answer.

"They're not that bad at the office."

Tyler looked at him with a you've-got-to-be-kidding-me expression.

Paul appeared sheepish. "Okay, not quite that bad. Really," he added, when she raised her eyebrows. She could pretend to be Paul's date but could never carry on the charade every working day. She never criticized him for his choices, and even though she didn't approve she could never let him down. They had gone through too much together.

"How's the new book coming?"

Tyler could always depend on her writing to take her away from everything. It was her escape, her visit to fantasy when reality sucked. And in the last few years it had more than sucked.

"I'm thinking about something and I can't decide which way to go with it." Paul was an excellent sounding board, and they would spend hours on the phone when she was trying to work through a scene or needed a specific word or phrase.

"Tell Mr. Muse." Paul handed her a cold beer.

Tyler couldn't help but laugh. Paul knew how to take the edge off the situation, and between her fellow guests at dinner and the change in her reaction to Kristin, she definitely needed it.

"I can't decide if Blake comes out of the closet in this book."

"What?" Paul asked, obviously shocked.

In Tyler's mind Blake was a lesbian, but what she had always kept her character's sexual preference vague. The lesbians embraced her, her mainstream publishing house never asked, and the fan-fic sites speculated. Blake's character had developed over the series and, with such a strong fan base, it was time. At least Tyler thought so.

"Have you discussed this with Roberta?"

"No." Tyler was taking a don't-ask-don't-tell approach with her editor. Roberta wouldn't know until she reached chapter twenty-eight. Tyler suspected she would suggest a rewrite of the final two chapters, but Tyler wasn't going to do it. She was tired of tiptoeing around the subject of Blake's sexuality. It wasn't as if it were a traditional romance, for crying out loud, and her readers were expecting Blake to marry, pop out a few kids, and live happily ever after in suburbia. Blake would never be tied to convention unless she wanted to. She told Paul as much.

"That's pretty gutsy, Tyler. Roberta's going to shit a brick." Paul had met Roberta when he attended a few of her book signings, and he'd hit her reaction right on the money.

"Well, she shouldn't," Tyler replied, suddenly very tired of the façade. Between her personal situation, her sudden attraction to Kristin this evening, and the trip this coming week, the pressure was starting to build.

❖

"What in the fuck was that about? 'Thanks for the conversation, Kristin.'" Steven mocked Tyler's words.

Kristin recoiled inside but fought to keep her feet firmly anchored to the floor. Steven often acted like this after one of their dinner parties. She didn't look at him, knowing she'd see the fire in his eyes. She thought she'd seen a much different kind of fire in Tyler's earlier but couldn't think about that right now.

"Steven, you know I was just making polite small talk for our guests. I always do. I was simply keeping the conversation going."

She used her calmest, most acquiescent tone, hoping it would do the trick. She never knew with him anymore.

"Really?" he asked, as if trying to catch her in something. "What did she have to say? I can't believe she has the nerve to sit with us and voice her opinion on what we're discussing. What the fuck does she know? She calls herself a writer, for God's sake. She probably can't get a real job."

Steven had never read one of Tyler's books and never would. Kristin couldn't remember the last time he'd read anything other than a financial report.

"It was just conversation, Steven. I wasn't soliciting her political views." Kristin knew she'd stepped over the line when Steven inhaled sharply.

"She's an aggressive bitch, Kristin, and I don't want you anywhere near her."

Kristin replied cautiously. "That might be difficult since we'll all be on the island together."

"You're the one that invited her," Steven shot back. His breath smelled like too much whiskey and she knew what that meant.

"How could we not? You know she and Paul are together. We couldn't invite just him and exclude her. It wouldn't look right." That would calm him down. Steven was nothing but predictable when it came to how things "looked." Too bad he didn't worry about how *he* looked. His shirt was one size too small, and he hadn't seen his belt buckle in years.

"She's got more balls than Paul and a man's name. I bet I know who's on top in that bedroom." Steven sneered and finally walked away. Before he got too far he turned and said, "I want to have sex tonight. Turn out the lights and come to bed."

CHAPTER FOUR

Tell me again why I'm doing this?"

"Because you love me, adore me, and will do anything for me."

Tyler had to laugh. "Yeah, right, lover boy. You and what hot lesbian do you have in that Gucci suitcase?" Tyler asked, pointing at his luggage. "My God, Paul, we won't even be gone a week. What in the hell did you pack?" Tyler bumped her hip against Paul as they walked from the parking lot to the hangar. He was carrying two suitcases and a garment bag over his shoulder whereas she had a duffle bag, a backpack, and her laptop.

"Hey, don't mess with me. I just might leave you on that island."

"Promise?" Tyler was teasing but felt a stab of guilt at the truth in her statement. At times she'd like nothing better than to disappear and not have to face her life. Less often now than a few years ago, but the longing still crept in when she was stressed. Like this trip. She shook off the feeling and held the door as Paul squeezed himself and his entire wardrobe through the door.

They were the last to arrive, and even though they weren't late, Steven's scowl indicated he thought otherwise. Paul placed his luggage next to the others', reached for Tyler's, and left her with her laptop case. She had spent most of the weekend writing and was on what she called her writer's roll, often producing five or six thousand words a day. She never went anywhere without at least a notebook and pen in her pocket.

Tyler glanced around the small waiting area looking for a place to sit. She had tossed and turned all night and her leg was already killing her. At only eight thirty in the morning that was unusual, and she'd taken a pain pill with breakfast. The remaining twenty-nine were in the bottle in her backpack.

The Starfields and the Browns sat next to each other, the men reading the day's *Wall Street Journal*. What would happen to them after a week without the prestigious paper? *WSJ* withdrawal might become a new mental illness.

Robert wore what looked like the same conservative business clothes he had on for the dinner party, except no tie or jacket. He hadn't even rolled up his long sleeves a cuff, and his wingtips looked as spit-shined as usual. Patty and Joan looked like they were going on a yachting cruise, not to an island of sand and surf. At least Mark was wearing a polo shirt, though starched within an inch of its life.

The only one dressed appropriately for this ridiculous adventure was Kristin. Her white cotton drawstring pants looked practical, yet elegant, as did the contrasting jade-green, scoop-neck T-shirt accentuating her eyes. Her flat-heel sandals were silent when she quickly walked across the room to greet them.

Thank God somebody dressed for the occasion, Kristin thought as she approached Tyler. Tyler was wearing khaki trousers held up with a thin black belt, white tennis shoes, and a short-sleeve shirt with some type of tropical print. Sunglasses hung around her neck, and a large blue sport watch was wrapped around her left wrist. Seeing Tyler in casual wear took her breath away.

Paul spoke to her, and Kristin blinked a few times to banish the mental image of Tyler transformed into her character Blake. They exchanged a few words before Steven walked into the room and took over.

Kristin watched Tyler as Steven gave last-minute instructions about the flight. Tyler was sitting next to Paul, and a vision of Tyler in the throes of passion burst into Kristin's head. She coughed a few times to shake it away. The comment Steven made the other night about Tyler and Paul together must have caused it.

She had often wondered why Tyler and Paul weren't married. As far as she could tell, they'd been together for years and she was obviously devoted to him. Why else would she be with Paul at every politically required social event and put up with Steven for this long? Maybe because they lived in separate states? No, that wasn't it. It didn't make sense. Tyler was an author and could write anywhere.

And her limp. She had noticed it the first time they'd met and thought it was the result of a simple injury. Maybe a sprained ankle or pulled muscle. But she limped every time Kristin saw her and didn't appear self-conscious about it. What had happened? An accident? She couldn't find any information about it anywhere on the Web. Tyler intrigued her, and Kristin was surprised at how very much she was looking forward to this week.

❖

"Does he rule over meetings like this?" Tyler whispered to Paul. Steven had been going on and on about something for over half an hour. After the first few minutes Tyler's mind had started to drift as Steven droned on about their final destination, a small private island near the Marshall Islands.

"Depends," Paul replied, sounding equally bored.

Finally Steven wrapped it up, clapping his chubby hands twice. "All right, everybody, let's saddle up."

Tyler looked at Paul as if to say "Is he serious?" Thankfully Paul didn't say anything but rolled his eyes in agreement.

They followed the others through the small door and into a large hangar. The jet bore the familiar logo of Learjet, one of the most prestigious personal and business jets in the world. Thin red and gray stripes streaked from the tip of the plane, under each of the eight windows, and ended just past the wings. The lettering on the bright-red tail section indicated this was the Learjet 852, the latest, most luxurious model, and Tyler was impressed. She had flown on an earlier model during her last book tour and had been gaga over its amenities and comfort. She had read about the 852 in a brochure at the airport while waiting for her flight in San

Francisco. The open door of the gleaming white plane beckoned them aboard.

Steven boarded first, the unfolded steps swaying as he climbed. Tyler thought she heard the plane groan under his weight. Patty Starfield followed Steven, the Browns behind them, proceeding in single file up the narrow steps. Tyler hesitated and motioned to Kristin to go first.

"No, go ahead, after you," she said, looking at both Tyler and Paul. "You're the guests."

Kristin's smile was polite yet Tyler detected it was only on the surface. Tyler didn't envy Kristin. She was married to an asshole, had to entertain six virtual strangers for a week, and if the dark circles under her eyes were any indication, she was already exhausted.

"You need to stop thinking like that, Kristin." This was one of the few times Tyler actually spoke Kristin's name, and it sounded better than any other time. "I hope you don't think you need to wait on us hand and foot. It'll be a long week if you do. We're all adults. We can take care of ourselves." Even if the other five don't believe it, she thought.

Kristin shot a quick glance toward the plane before answering. "Nonsense, you're our guests. Now let's get aboard, shall we? I'm sure Steven's ready to go."

Kristin motioned toward the steps and Tyler felt Kristin's eyes on her as she ascended. She had to stoop to enter the plane, her height exceeding that of the doorway. She hadn't seen any of the other women duck and didn't think five foot nine was unusually tall.

Two steps in and Tyler saw that this plane screamed money—serious money. Her senses kicked into overdrive when she smelled expensive leather. Thick carpet muffled any sound as she walked farther into the cabin. On her left Mark and Robert and their wives sat in four large leather seats facing each other, Mark's long legs spilling into the aisle. A blistering-white table edged in gleaming wood-grain trim separated the couples. An equally plush seat across the narrow aisle, a lone soldier, waited for an occupant. The third row contained only two seats, and behind that another set of four seats mirrored the first two rows. Was it her imagination or were she and Paul being snubbed in a posh, polite manner?

Because the interior was higher than the doorway, Tyler was able to walk down the aisle to the open seats without trouble. Paul wanted the window seat, and after stowing her laptop bag, Tyler settled into the buttery-soft white leather and buckled her seat belt. Kristin stepped into the plane and directly into the cockpit.

Kristin didn't close the door behind her, and even though Tyler couldn't hear the words being exchanged, Kristin's body language said they weren't pleasant. An unfamiliar urge to go to Kristin's rescue swept over Tyler and she tamped it down. That was none of her business. As Paul's "significant other" she had a role to play, which didn't include marriage counselor, referee, or knight in shining armor.

A few minutes later, Kristin came down the aisle appearing a little more frayed around the edges than earlier. When she looked at her, Tyler gave Kristin her most encouraging smile as the engines fired up.

The takeoff was smooth, the powerful Pratt & Whitney engines lifting them into the sky effortlessly. They banked to the left and before long reached their cruising altitude.

Tyler pressed the panel where the audio and video controls were hidden. The panel popped open, revealing controls for a DVD player, XM satellite radio, and access points to charge a variety of personal devices. Individual lighting above the table would be ideal if she decided to work on her next book, and the reading light over her right shoulder was perfect if she wanted to disappear into someone else's.

The clink of Kristin unbuckling her seat belt drew Tyler's attention from her electronic control panel as Kristin walked up the aisle toward the front of the cabin. She was thin, too thin, but the natural sway of her hips attractive just the same.

Kristin held her breath as she approached the cockpit. Steven had been in a foul mood after their dinner guests left the night before last and had taken it out on her, as was his modus operandi these last few years.

He wasn't physical but preferred to use his sharp tongue to inflict damage. Lately, though, Kristin wasn't quite sure it would continue to be that way. He wouldn't do or say anything inappropriate in front of his staff. He never had, just stored it up for when they were alone and he felt like unleashing it.

It hadn't always been like this. In the beginning Steven was everything a woman dreamed of in a husband—considerate, kind, and accommodating. By all accounts they were the perfect couple. The comments and innuendos that accompanied marrying the only child of one of the largest real-estate developers in the country didn't seem to bother Steven. He loved her, not her money. He was a successful commodities trader and had built a nice nest egg of his own. He didn't need hers. But once he gained control of PPH Development, everything changed.

During the first few years of their marriage, unbeknownst to anyone, including Kristin and her family, Steven bought out her father's first partner, then had enough shares from the second that he controlled the entire company. And before long he assumed unquestionable control: over PPH, her family's future, and her.

One night after their dinner guests had left Steven told her he didn't want her to work anymore. She was stunned. She was the vice president of environmental regulations at PPH and had been since graduating from business school. She and her staff of twelve were responsible for anything relating to the environment at any PPH site around the world. She often dealt with groundwater issues, easements, city engineers, and once a toxic-waste dump on PPH-owned land.

She remembered it as if it were yesterday and not six years ago.

"I beg your pardon?" Kristin wasn't sure she had heard him correctly over the clatter of dishes she was loading into the dishwasher.

"You heard me. I don't want you working." His voice was sharper than Kristin had ever heard it.

"Where did that come from?" Kristin asked, stopping before she rinsed the last plate.

"It didn't come from anywhere. I never wanted you to work."

Kristin was shocked. Steven had never expressed anything other than total support of her career. She stared at him and realized that he was dead serious. Something was up and she had no idea what.

"What are you talking about? I love my job, and I'm damn good at it. Last week the US Department of Agriculture asked me to be the keynote speaker at their annual leadership meeting."

"No."

Kristin's hands started to shake. "What do you mean no? I've already said yes."

"Then tell them no." His voice had gone from sharp to so calm it was cold.

Steven hadn't moved from where he sat on the stool by the counter since this bizarre conversation began. He had hardly blinked and Kristin didn't like the look in his eyes.

Kristin set the plate in the sink, dried her hands, and said, "What's going on with you, Steven? You've never had a problem with my job before."

"That's before I was the majority owner of PPH."

For the second time in almost as many minutes, Kristin wasn't sure what she'd just heard. "What?"

"Do you need to get your hearing checked?" Steven said, a little less calmly than a moment ago. As a matter of fact it sounded almost nasty. "I said, I am the majority owner of PPH and my wife is not working." He separated the last few words with a slight pause for emphasis.

Kristin was stunned. She knew one of her father's partners had recently sold his share of the business, but not to Steven, she was certain. His next words showed just how wrong she was.

"I'm Davenport Holdings," Steven said cockily.

"What?" Kristin couldn't say anything more, her shock and disbelief overwhelming her.

"If all you can say is *what*, then you're stupider than I thought." This time Steven mocked her.

Kristin felt her mouth drop open and her world start to slide. She gripped the edge of the counter for support. "But that was only Kenneth's share," she said, naming her father's now ex-partner.

Steven got up and calmly walked over to within an arm's length in front of her. She smelled the scotch on his breath and his expression frightened her.

"One and three quarters beats one and one quarter anytime," he said with a sneer. "And Oscar," Steven named her father's other partner, "Oscar heard that ol' Kenny boy got such a great deal he sold half of his share to Davenport. He signed the papers this afternoon." He stepped closer and Kristin fought not to recoil. "Do the math, sweetheart. PPH is mine." Steven started to move away, then changed his mind. "Oh, and another thing. They took shares of Davenport instead of cash, and I can turn them into worthless paper in an instant." He snapped his fingers to emphasize his point.

Kristin was speechless. If what Steven said was true, he owned controlling interest in PPH. He could do whatever he wanted with the company her family had built and was depending on for their future, their retirement. And he could ruin them as well. She felt sick to her stomach.

This time he did walk away, but not before adding, "Oh, and if you try to divorce me or take me to court or anything else you can think of that would upset me, including talking eco-green-peace crap to a bunch of overpaid bureaucrats, I'll do it, in a heartbeat." He snapped his fingers again and left Kristin staring at his retreating back.

She quietly hired an attorney, who, in turn, hired a forensic accountant, and a month later she was sitting across the wide oak table in the attorney's office in shock. That was six years and a lifetime ago.

She never said anything of Steven's threats to her parents as Steven not so quietly assumed control of PPH. Her father had already had two heart attacks, and a third would be his last. Her mother had married Gil Porter when she was eighteen and would be lost without him, so Kristin did as Steven said and tried not to rock too many boats.

She squared her shoulders as she approached Steven, his large body filling the small cabin.

"Would you like something to drink?" she asked, glancing around the cockpit, her eyes landing on the brightly lit instrument panel. She was more familiar with Mars than the knobs and gauges on the controls in front of him.

Steven barked out a command for a coffee, not looking at her. "And make sure everyone has enough booze in them so they'll sleep for an hour or two. We're going to hit some bad weather, and if they're asleep they won't even notice." Steven grumbled and scratched the back of his neck.

"A drink? Steven, it's not even ten o'clock." She glanced at the Timex on her wrist. Steven insisted on her always wearing the Rolex he had given her last year, and when she emerged from the bedroom this morning wearing her favorite watch, he'd been furious. He hated it.

"What is that piece of shit?" he'd growled, looking at her black, scuffed timepiece. His nose crinkled as if he had a mouth full of something distasteful.

"Steven, you don't expect me to wear a ten-thousand-dollar watch on the island, do you? It might get scratched or even lost. You wouldn't want that to happen, would you?" She had appealed to his idea of appearance, knowing it worked better than outright defiance. He didn't say anything but grunted and turned away.

"Is the weather going to be bad? Can we fly around it?" Kristin asked, never comfortable with anything other than her two feet on solid ground.

Steven, his face beet-red, spun around and she immediately regretted her words. "Don't you tell me what to do. I'm the one flying this piece of gold, and I know what I'm doing. Now go and be a good little stewardess and ask if they'd like coffee, tea, or me." He chuckled, a sinister laugh Kristin had never heard before. "On second thought, sweetheart, don't bother. Nobody would take you up on that last one." Steven turned, effectively dismissing her, his attention back to the open sky in front of them.

Kristin didn't cry. She didn't cringe, cower, or say anything. After she recovered from the shock of Steven's bombshell years ago she felt nothing. Absolutely nothing. She simply backed out of the doorway and into the small galley.

She pulled down several crystal glasses and filled them with ice. She tucked an assortment of snacks, courtesy of airport catering, into a cloth-lined basket and stepped back into the main cabin.

In the first row, Mark was reading the latest book about Bernie Madoff's ponzi empire while Patty flipped through the latest issue of *Glamour*, her manicured fingernails snapping each page. Across from them Robert gazed out the window, and Joan held a catalogue from Williams-Sonoma in her lap. The first time Kristin and Steven were at the Browns' for dinner she had a vague sense of deja vu as she sat in their living room. It nagged at her until one day when she was throwing away an old copy of a WS catalogue left in the guest room. It slipped from her hand and landed on the floor open to a picture of a slightly different room decorated with the same items as she had seen in Joan and Robert's living room. It was almost a perfect replica. How unoriginal.

"Would you like something to eat or drink?" Kristin offered the basket of snacks. Her voice must have sounded the same because no one gave her a second look, simply taking a granola bar and asking for coffee. God, she felt like a glorified waitress. But wasn't that what she really was? Always making sure her husband and his business cronies had everything they needed? She didn't know if it was worse with his business associates or with his employees, both of whom he simply had to impress.

In the early years of their marriage Kristin had loved entertaining Steven's associates. The small dinners with one or two other couples grew to be dinner parties for dozens along with her ability to manage them herself. Actually it wasn't long after Steven's first promotion that he told her he didn't want her doing anything in the kitchen while they had guests, and he preferred to have the meal catered. He said it freed her from the kitchen drudgery, and at first Kristin was thrilled. Then after the fourth or twenty-fourth or whatever number they were on now, she wished she could disappear into the kitchen.

Steven's associates were boors, chauvinists, and egotistical bastards. During one such party years ago Kristin had finally realized that her husband was one as well. When did that happen?

She never would have allowed him to be that way. Yeah, right, and how long had it been since she'd had any say in anything with him? The most unsettling was how some of the men looked at her when Steven wasn't looking at them. They gave her the creeps, and if not for some careful maneuvering one evening, she would have found herself in a difficult situation. Some men were just plain pigs clad in Armani suits.

Kristin told herself to put on her happy face, but when her eyes met Tyler's she knew she wasn't in time. Tyler was frowning and her blue eyes bored into hers. Kristin pretended nothing was wrong.

"Tyler, Paul." She addressed them a little too enthusiastically. "Would you two like a snack and something to drink?"

Tyler quickly unbuckled her seat belt and stood, forcing Kristin to step back.

"We'll just have some coffee, thanks. I can get it."

Kristin had never been this close to Tyler, the small cabin not leaving much room for anything else. Tyler was taller than her by more than a few inches, putting her eyes directly in the line of sight of Tyler's lips. For the first time Kristin noticed how full and perfectly formed they were and detected a pale scar, about an inch long, above her top lip. She wanted to trace her tongue over it. The cabin suddenly felt very, very small.

Kristin stumbled backward, shocked at the thought so clear in her mind. What had gotten into her? She had never thought of Tyler, or any woman for that matter, that way. At least not in twenty years, that is.

Tyler grabbed her arm before she could escape, steadying her. Tyler's hand was hot on her skin and Kristin stared at it, fully expecting to see smoke.

"Are you all right?" Tyler's voice was soft and low.

Kristin glanced around quickly, relieved that only Paul was aware of what had just happened. The sound of Tyler's voice drew her eyes away from the tan hand to look again into her eyes. What she saw this time took her breath away. Tyler's eyes were filled with something she couldn't describe, and they flashed quickly before returning to their normal pale blue.

"Yes, thank you. We must have hit a bump." Somehow Kristin found her voice but it didn't sound anything like her. Tyler still had not removed her hand from her arm, and Kristin never wanted her to. Tyler looked at her hand, then back at Kristin. She didn't say anything for what felt to Kristin like an eternity. Then Tyler let go of her arm quickly, as if the heat that was racing through Kristin's body had scorched her.

"Let me help," Tyler said, her voice a bit rough. She motioned in the direction of the galley.

"That's not necessary," Kristin replied, ever the good hostess.

"What's not necessary is for you to wait on us," Tyler replied. "We're all perfectly capable of getting our own coffee." She glanced at her fellow passengers. "At least I am," she added with a smile.

Tyler's smile was dazzling. Kristin had seen her smile before, but more out of politeness rather than joy, she realized. This was different. Before she had a chance to reply, Tyler spoke.

"Come on, I insist." She started moving forward, Kristin not having any alternative but to go as well.

As they walked the few steps up the aisle Kristin felt Tyler's eyes on her. Heat started behind her neck, moved down her back, over her butt, and settled between her legs. What was happening? She had been with Tyler on many occasions, sitting next to her or across from her, their fingers occasionally touching when passing a plate or transferring a wineglass. And she shook Tyler's hand when she arrived at whatever event they were attending and when she left. It wasn't as if she'd never touched her before. But why this reaction? Why now?

CHAPTER FIVE

Don't do it. Do not do it, Tyler told herself as she watched Kristin walk up the aisle in front of her. She never was one for listening to her inner voice—the one that told her not to eat that third doughnut or look down the front of a beautiful woman's blouse. Especially the voice telling her not to cruise the wife of her best friend's boss. Tyler swallowed, knowing good and well this wasn't the right thing to do. And certainly not in the tight confines of a private plane jetting to a tropical island for five days. Not the *right* thing? Hell, it wasn't the *smart* thing either.

Kristin protested again. "I told you, you don't have to do this." She glanced nervously toward the open cockpit door.

"I know you did. And I said I can take care of myself. That, and I'm training Paul as well. His mother waited on him hand and foot as a child." Her comment was far from the truth but Kristin didn't need to know that. "So far I'm doing pretty good except for morning coffee," Tyler added, trying to ease a little humor into the conversation. The tension in the air thickened as they walked closer to the front of the plane.

"Good for you. Don't let him—" Steven barked for coffee from the cockpit.

Kristin stiffened and Tyler wanted to step in front of her and tell Steven to get off his ass and get it himself. But he was flying the plane so she assumed he couldn't very well leave the cockpit unattended. At least he could have said please.

Kristin didn't make eye contact with Tyler but simply poured some of the hot liquid in a stainless-steel travel mug embossed with the company logo. When she did finally look at her, her face was strained, her smile tight. Kristin didn't say anything as she turned and entered the cockpit.

Tyler poured two cups of coffee, the muffled sound of Steven's harsh voice coming from her left. She couldn't make out the conversation, but nothing good ever comes from between clenched teeth. Wanting to make sure Kristin was okay, Tyler stalled, but when it was apparent it would look odd if she stood there too long, Tyler took her cups and went to sit back down next to Paul.

"What's with them?" Tyler asked Paul quietly, handing over his coffee.

"Who?" He looked up from the magazine he was reading and glanced around.

"Sometimes you're absolutely clueless, Paul." Tyler sighed good-naturedly. "Your boss and his beautiful wife." Her comment sneaked out before she knew it, and when Paul raised his eyebrows, Tyler knew it didn't slip by him.

"Don't say it, don't even think it," Tyler replied too quickly. "I just asked what's with them." Kristin exited the cockpit and began serving the others their beverage without looking at her. Tyler noticed the strain on her face again.

"No," Paul said emphatically, bringing her attention back to their conversation. "You asked what's with my boss and his beautiful wife. And I emphasize that you used the word *beautiful*." Paul blew on his coffee before carefully sipping it.

"Stop it, Paul," Tyler warned him. "We are not going there. Certainly not on this trip and definitely not in this can with all these big ears around."

"Nobody's listening, and when are you going to accept that it's time to move on?" Paul did lean closer and spoke a little softer.

"Are you out of your mind talking about this now? Here?" Tyler asked, indicating their cramped surroundings with a wave of her hand. "I don't care who knows I'm a lesbian, but isn't the whole point of this outlandish charade that nobody else does?"

"If it means you'll finally get out and go on a real date I'll gladly shout from the rooftops that you're back on the market," Paul said seriously.

"Paul," Tyler said. It had been several months since they'd had this conversation, and she was hoping he'd just drop it. Wrong.

"Come on, Tyler. You're thirty-nine-years old, rich, talented, famous, and drop-dead gorgeous. Your life is not over. Your sex life is definitely not over. Or at least it shouldn't be. From what I read, women your age are just hitting their stride." Paul was an avid reader, but unfortunately for her he held *Psychology Today* right now.

Kristin came back down the aisle and Tyler wanted to turn around and see what she was doing but couldn't without being too obvious. "Paul, you have got to stop reading *Cosmo* and pick up an issue of *Field and Stream* now and then."

"Honey, fish stink, and you'll never find an article in *Cosmo* titled, 'When it's time to stop believing no one's going to want a woman with one leg.'"

"Is that the cover story this month?" Tyler asked, a little too sharply.

"No, but I bet if I wrote about you and sent it in, it would be." Paul's blue eyes softened. "Tyler, Jessica is an ass. You know it, I know it, and all your friends knew it."

"Paul," Tyler said, not wanting to talk about this subject again. She was tired of fighting about it. "This is not about Jessica."

"The hell it isn't," Paul said through gritted teeth. "Jessica left you. She walked out on you because she's stupid, shallow, and a C-U-Next-Tuesday." Tyler couldn't help but smile at Paul's choice of words. "And that 'It's me, not you' bullshit was probably the only truthful thing she ever said. She's a cowardly, narcissistic, self-centered bitch."

"Jesus, Paul, how do you really feel?" Tyler knew Paul didn't care much for Jessica but had tactfully kept his opinions to himself. Luckily they all weren't together that often, with Tyler and Jessica in San Francisco and Paul in Houston.

She and Jessica hadn't been in a relationship that consisted of two dogs, matching rings, and a mortgage, but they were monogamous and had exchanged the magical three words. A variety of factors kept them from being more than that.

First, Tyler owned an apartment in the city that barely had enough room for her, let alone another person and all her worldly possessions. Second, Tyler loved her "alone time," as she called it. It was when she retreated into the world of her characters and sometimes didn't emerge for hours, if not days. The fact that Jessica lived and worked in Oakland and had made it very clear that she wasn't interested in an everyday commute was another. So, they saw each other occasionally during the week and on most weekends. They were a couple who cared about each other. At least Tyler had thought they did.

Paul continued firmly. "When was the last time you asked a woman out to dinner, went for a walk, or did anything but have a quick fuck with your clothes on? Just because you lost part of a leg doesn't mean you're any less the woman you were before the accident."

"You forget about the eleven-inch scar on my stomach," Tyler added bitterly, her pain still simmering just below the surface. Paul was right. She hadn't had sex with a woman that wasn't fast, hard, just this side of anonymous, and never, ever naked.

"Double bullshit," Paul replied, waving his hand as if her comment wasn't worth the time. "You almost died, Tyler. If that car had been an inch closer you would have. You're lucky you only lost your leg and a few feet of your guts. And for Jessica to leave you because you can't walk as fast, scale mountains in a single bound, or whatever physical thing you dykes do when you get together is just stupid."

Paul looked at her. Even after five years she still saw the frightened expression in his eyes when he talked about her accident. She and Jessica were jogging when a man, drunk at seven fifteen in the morning, had jumped the curb and hit Tyler. She lost her left leg just above the knee, her spleen, and some of her intestines. Jessica didn't even get a scratch. "You could have died," he said quietly.

Tyler took his hand. "I know, buddy, and I'm glad I didn't." In one of her few moments of self-pity, she had confided in Paul that shortly after she came home from the hospital Jessica told her that her scar and stump were a complete turnoff and hadn't touched her after the accident. Jessica barely gave her the courtesy of simply telling her. Tyler took a calming breath. "But it still hurts to know I didn't see that in her. We were together two years and she never gave me any indication she would do that."

"Aren't you glad you didn't do the white-picket-fence thing?"

Tyler smiled at the laughter in his voice and the grin on his face. "Do I look like the white-picket-fence kind of lesbian?" She lowered her voice to an almost-whisper for the last word.

"Actually Blake could find ten things to do with that picket, and I expect to read about every one in the next book." Paul took her hand. "Tyler, I love you and just want you to be happy."

Kristin chose that moment to walk by, her pants lightly brushing Tyler's arm as she passed. The scent of lilacs hung in the air. Tyler watched her settle into the seat across the aisle and one row up. Heard the seat belt snap. Saw her long legs cross, the bottom of her pants creep up to reveal tan ankles.

"I am happy," Tyler replied. Tyler saw the slight tremble of Kristin's hand as she raised her coffee cup to her lips. *Liar.*

CHAPTER SIX

W e're gonna crash!"
Steven's voice echoed through the small cabin with
the same panicked high pitch as it had not five minutes earlier when
he announced a problem with the hydraulics. They were making an
emergency landing.

Tyler double-checked her seat belt, pulling it even tighter than
she had the first time she heard they were in trouble. Paul, sitting
beside her, repeated her movements and included the sign of the
cross across his chest as his contribution to their safe landing.

Tyler was a veteran flyer and often wondered how she'd react
in this situation. She'd always thought she'd be calm, or at least
hoped she would, but you never really knew how you'd react until
faced with just this situation. So far so good, she thought. Although
her heart was beating faster than normal she was calm, unlike the
other occupants of the jet, including, by the sound of it, their captain.

Thirty minutes earlier they had run into a storm, rain pelting
the exterior of the plane, wind gusts pitching them across the sky.
Tyler had a strong stomach, but during one rough patch she'd started
looking for the barf bag. Steven had come on the speakers overhead,
reassuring them that they would be through the worst of it in a few
more minutes. Sometime between that announcement and now,
something had gone terribly wrong.

Across the aisle Kristin, pale, stared straight ahead while she
gripped the arms of the leather chair. Tyler didn't bother to look at the

others. She suspected their expressions were similar to Kristin's—scared shitless. At least the screams in front of her had stopped. In the tight confines of the plane the screams had pierced her ears like an ice pick through butter. If not for the fact that she might be killed, she had been tempted to unfasten her seat belt and slap one of the women across the mouth to shut her up.

"Shit, don't let me die." Paul's deep voice echoed the words in her head.

"Ditto, big guy," Tyler replied, uttering the nickname for Paul she hadn't used in years.

The plane bucked to the left, the familiar screams starting again. Tyler felt oddly detached from what was going on around her. She expected to see her life flash before her eyes.

Where were the images of her childhood riding on the shoulders of her father up the stairs every night when he tucked her and her three brothers into bed? Where was her winning the science project in sixth grade? Standing in front of her fellow high-school students campaigning for equal rights for gays and lesbians in 1988? Where were the faces of Alice, Mary, Claudia, and all the other women that had passed through her life, some more quickly than others? Where was Jessica? Where was the accident, the one that had left her the way she was today and made her the woman she had become? Those thoughts flashed through her mind in three or four seconds as the jet fell out of the sky toward the water visible outside the window.

Tyler wasn't deeply religious but occasionally thought about what it might be like on the other side, wherever that might be. Would a bright, shining light lead toward a door? Would she need a key to open it and not have one? Would she find rolling hills covered in daisies or grains of wheat swaying in the summer breeze? Or would it be dark, filled with nothing? Would her little sister be there? Would she see her mother again after all these years? Would her little dog Bosco, the one that the school bus ran over one terrible day when she was eight, be there to greet her with his wet tongue and wagging tail? All these random thoughts skittered through her brain an instant before the plane staggered to a stop.

❖

Her chest hurt, making it difficult to breathe. Tyler felt like she was coming up from under water, rising slowly to the surface. She heard sounds around her, but they were muffled and she couldn't make out anything clearly. She tried to move her arms and didn't know if they actually didn't move or if she just couldn't feel them. She opened her eyes. No, check that, she tried to open her eyes, but her eyelids felt as heavy as the immense weight in her chest. She swallowed a few times, her mouth and throat completely dry. She coughed, something hot and sticky in her lungs.

We crashed. I'm alive. At least I think I'm alive. She commanded her eyelids to lift, turning her head at the same time, immediately stopping when a searing pain shot through her neck. She waited until the nausea that threatened to toss her breakfast settled. More cautiously this time she opened her eyes, blinking several times to clear her vision.

Reaching to her right she touched flesh. Paul. At least she hoped it was him. "Paul." Her voice sounded scratchy. She repeated his name, louder this time, the pain in her head intensifying. She moved her hand and recognized an arm and continued moving it until she found a hand and grasped it, interlocking their fingers. She squeezed tight. Carefully she turned her head to the side. "Paul, Paul, wake up." She felt his wrist, his pulse strong and steady. A sigh of relief made her chest hurt again.

After several careful shallow breaths her head cleared, and she became more aware of her surroundings. It was quiet. Thank God for that. Joan had finally stopped screaming. She didn't hear any popping or cracking from fire, which was one less thing to worry about. She didn't feel any water lapping around her ankle, or any other part of her body, for that matter. At least she wouldn't drown, not at this particular point in time. She remembered Steven screaming that the plane was going to crash, then seeing the crystal-clear blue water of the Pacific Ocean out the small window.

Risking searing pain again, she turned her head and looked out the small window, relieved to see blue sky. A second later, blue water rose and fell against the outside of the window as the plane rocked in the wave. Her relief was short-lived when she realized the jet was floating on top of the water, just waiting for the right moment to sink.

Movement to her left caught her attention. Kristin was slumped in her chair, head between her knees, arms dangling on either side of her legs. Tyler didn't see any blood, but its absence could signal internal injuries.

Tyler carefully lifted her head as much as possible in the tight confines of her seating area. Emergency oxygen masks dangled from the ceiling, reminding her of moss that hung suspended over the murky bayous in her native Louisiana. She didn't remember the masks dropping, but she didn't think the cabin had depressurized enough to trigger the ejection of the life-saving apparatus. They must have popped open on impact.

A barely audible sound came from Paul, and her heart leapt for joy. She didn't think he was injured, but until he woke up she couldn't be sure. He lifted his head and opened his eyes, blinking several times.

"Paul, I'm right here, big guy." Tyler was absolutely relieved.

"What happened?" He blinked a half-dozen more times before his foggy eyes began to clear.

"We crashed. But you're all right. I'm all right," she added quickly. "Really, we're okay."

"Crashed?" Paul asked, looking around, obviously surprised at the devastation inside the plane. "All I remember is Steven screaming at us."

"Yeah, well, that's about it up to this point. We're in the water. We've got to get our survivor asses out of this plane."

Tyler unbuckled her seat belt and double-checked that all her limbs were in working condition. Assured everything was operating as designed, she reached across Paul, undid his buckle, and helped him stand.

Stars flashed behind Tyler's eyes. She fought against the blackness threatening to overtake her remaining vision and took a deep breath, holding on to the back of the seat in front of her. Paul did the same, giving her a couple of seconds more to steady her legs.

"You okay?" he asked.

"I think so. I'm a little woozy, things are a little blurry, but I'll be all right." Tyler answered more to convince herself than Paul. She looked at the carnage around her.

Patty sat in her seat, eyes wide open, and Tyler didn't know if she was dead or simply in shock. Her husband Mark slumped against her. Blood was dripping from Robert's nose, and Joan was wiping it with a paper napkin, her face paler than ever.

"How is everybody else?" Paul asked, concerned about his associates.

"I saw Kristin move a couple of minutes ago."

Paul turned to look at his boss's wife just at the moment she started to sit up. She grasped her head, moaning softly.

"I'm not sure about Patty." Tyler referenced the woman who had sat in front of her in the first row. "She's breathing but look at that huge knot on her head."

Paul shuddered when he looked around again.

"Come on," Tyler said, taking Paul's arm. She wondered how much movement it would take before the plane started to sink.

"We've got to get out of here."

CHAPTER SEVEN

K ristin gasped when the plane rocked as Tyler slowly
walked down the aisle. She was trying to be careful and
not to make any sudden movement for fear the fuselage would crack
open, sending them to the bottom of the ocean.

"What are you doing?" Robert barked from behind her as Joan
shrieked again.

Tyler stopped and looked at Kristin, then at Robert, blood drops
on his long white sleeve. "We can't stay here. We've got to figure
out how to get out." Tyler looked around trying to determine just
how long they'd have when the door opened. She saw a beach out
the windows on the left side and it didn't look too far away.

"You're going to get us killed. We should just sit still until
we're rescued. Let the professionals handle it."

Spoken like a true Republican lawyer, Tyler thought, but kept
her opinion to herself. This time she did turn to face Robert. "We've
got to at least try, Robert. Several of us are hurt, a few seriously,
and we can't just sit here and wait to sink. Because we *are* going to
sink."

"Nonsense," he replied with bluster. "This isn't one of your
books where your made-up main character invents some ingenious
way to get everyone out of a pickle. We've crashed, for God's sake.
This is reality."

"Which is exactly why we've got to get out of here." Tyler
started to move toward the front of the plane.

"The life jackets are under the seats." Kristin's voice was shaking but clear.

Tyler glanced at Kristin over her shoulder. The color was returning to her face, and she didn't look as shaken as she had a few minutes ago.

"How are we going to get out?" Kristin asked.

"The same way we came in. We've got to open the door before we go under or we won't be able to. The pressure will be too great." Tyler pulled the life jacket from under Mark's seat. "Here, put this on," she said, handing him the orange vest, which was almost the color of Joan's hair. "Get Patty's on too."

The plane groaned and rocked from side to side. Tyler looked at Kristin then to Paul, who said, "Get us the fuck out of this plane."

Before Tyler had a chance to turn the crank on the door Steven yelled from the cockpit. "What in the fuck is going on back there? Somebody get up here and help me. My leg's broken. Kristin?" His last three sentences ran together.

Kristin jerked her head in the direction of his voice. She hadn't even thought about him or worried if he had survived the crash. Steven hollered again.

"I know you're there, Kristin, I hear your voice. I need help, goddamnit. Robert, get up here."

"Just a minute, Steven," Kristin replied somewhat testily. She looked at Robert, indicating to him to stay put. It always amazed her how grown men actually jumped at Steven's command. But then again, didn't she? "We're trying to figure out how to get out without drowning."

"Well, hurry up. I'm in a lot of pain and there's glass all over the place."

Kristin was embarrassed, yet again, by her husband's all-about-me attitude. She looked around the opulent plane for the first time, and her stomach flipped when she saw the condition and its occupants.

Tyler laid her hand on her arm. "Just focus on what we can do, not on what we can't." Kristin gazed back into warm, dark eyes that understood and nodded.

"What do you need me to do?" Kristin asked, feeling stronger just by Tyler's quick look of assurance.

"Put a life vest on Steven. When we're all ready, we'll open the door. If we're lucky we'll have enough time to get everyone out, but we have to plan on more like a few minutes, if that."

One by one Tyler and Paul checked to make sure everyone's life vest was properly secured. Steven was by far the most vocal in his opinion of what they should do to get him out of the cockpit, and Kristin almost told him to simply shut up.

Other than securing Steven's life vest, as well as her own, Kristin had little to do to actually help. Tyler and Paul moved anything away from the door that would hamper their quick escape. Kristin thought the two of them worked well together and made a good team. They would be good together as husband and wife.

Tyler's command of the situation impressed Kristin. Since they crashed Tyler had become the de-facto leader, and if not for her assertiveness, they would probably all still be sitting in their seats waiting to be saved.

Mark regained consciousness and Kristin had to stand on her toes to help him with his life vest. Patty was groggy, and Robert continued to voice his opinion that they should stay put.

"Then stay, I don't care one way or the other," Tyler finally told him, effectively shutting him up. She looked at Paul, then at her as if to ask, "Ready?" Kristin nodded even though she was anything but.

It took both Tyler and Paul to turn the latch on the door. Fresh air rushed into the cabin. Kristin raised her hand to cover her eyes, the bright light streaming in through the now-open door. She held her breath, waiting for the cold seawater to rush in.

"All right, Robert, you first, like we discussed. Everybody stay calm and ease out of the plane into the water. No sudden movements. Swim around the plane and toward the beach. Stay together but not too close." For the third time Tyler repeated the instructions she had already given them. It was no easy feat, but somehow Mark and Paul got Steven out of the cockpit, his screams of pain echoing in the almost-deserted cabin. Thankfully, he quieted when they got him in the water.

When it was Kristin's turn to exit she stepped into the small doorway, looked down, and froze. It was only about two feet into the water but it felt like miles. She wasn't the best swimmer and, combined with her near-death experience, she was unable to move. She couldn't remember if she was even breathing.

"It's okay. Just focus on what you need to do." Tyler's voice was calm and reassuring in her right ear. She had repeated that phrase several times since they crashed and it worked every time. Until now. Kristin was immobilized with fear.

"That's it, just breathe. In, out, in, out," Tyler repeated, and Kristin followed her words. She had a death grip on the door opening and Tyler covered her hands with hers. They were warm, and Kristin immediately felt more secure than she had in a very long time.

"I'm right behind you," Tyler said. "We're going to do this together. I won't let anything happen to you." Kristin leaned back into Tyler, her fear subsiding more than a little. Other than Paul, they were the last ones in the plane. The bottom of it was filling with water with every swell of the waves. Kristin knew they had to get out, but her brain wasn't communicating with her body.

"I'm going to tell you what to do and then we'll do it together. Okay?" Kristin nodded, but her head felt more like a bobble head than attached to her neck.

"First, we're going to sit down on the floor and then just slide into the water. I'll be right behind you the entire time."

Tyler's voice was little more than a whisper in her ear when Kristin entered the cold water. The pressure of the seawater took her breath away, and she started to panic.

"That's right, nice and slow," Tyler said from behind her. Her voice was so calm and soothing Kristin immediately relaxed. Slowly they swam away from the listing plane and toward the shoreline.

"That wasn't so bad, was it?" Tyler asked as they waded ashore.

Kristin was shaking so bad she could hardly answer. She was still scared, but somewhere in the distance between the plane and the ground, she had become far too aware of Tyler's hard body behind her, her breath tickling her neck each time she spoke.

CHAPTER EIGHT

Where are you going?" Steven's question sounded more like an accusation than an inquiry.

"To look around. We might be here a few hours or a few days, and we need to know what, if anything, is through those trees and down the beach. We might need it." Or need to be prepared for it, she thought but didn't dare say out loud. Tyler glanced toward the trees. Would their outcome have been different if they'd set down on land?

They had been onshore for about thirty minutes when the plane sank. She thought of the movie *Titanic* and how the great ship's nose slid under, sending the tail section practically straight up, then disappearing into the water too. Thankfully they had landed in a place about twenty feet deep, and Paul and Mark had made several trips to the aircraft to retrieve as many usable items as possible before it sank. Mark's height made it difficult for him to move around the small cabin of the plane, and Tyler had held her breath as Paul handed him supplies, luggage, and anything else he could get that they might need. She didn't breathe normally until both were back on shore.

Tyler and Paul worked through their fellow passengers, making sure everybody was okay. The survivors, eight including her and Paul, were in various conditions: Steven's broken leg, one probable concussion, and various cuts and scrapes. The bruising from Robert's broken nose added a splash of color to the circles under his eyes. Kristin had a small cut on her head, and everyone was still a bit stunned and dazed. Patty sat in the sun, looking oblivious to their situation.

"We need to stay together," Mark said, his voice thick. His clothes were still wet and stuck to him like a second skin, accentuating his height.

"I'll take Paul with me. We won't go far." As far as Tyler was concerned, the discussion was over. Paul got up and, with one last glance at their fellow survivors, Tyler headed down the beach, Steven still bitching.

Once they were out of earshot Paul asked, "What do you think we'll find?"

Tyler almost stumbled in the soft sand and grabbed Paul's arm for support. "Probably more of this." She gestured at the sand and trees around them. "But I hope we find a Club Med with smooth sidewalks and a bar right around that bend." She pointed to a small segment of land jutting out from the rest of the island. "If we're really lucky we'll find a babbling brook or a Kodak-moment fresh waterfall."

"When did you get to be so witty in a crisis?" he asked, steadying her again.

"Occupational hazard. I'm trying to think of what Blake would do to get us out of this mess, and you know how quick her tongue is. And it's a defense mechanism, you know. Offense is better than defense."

Tyler turned around, checking to make sure they were out of sight. She stopped and practically fell into the warm sand. Paul looked at her, concerned. "I've got sand in my sleeve," she said. He knelt beside her.

"What can I do to help?"

God, she loved this guy. The minute Paul had heard about the accident, he cut short a business trip in Singapore and spent twenty hours on a plane just to sit with her in the hospital. For a week he held her hand, changed her bedpan, and read her to sleep. When her physical therapy began he pushed, cajoled, and even threatened her into not giving up on the excruciatingly painful rehabilitation. He was there when she took her first step on her new leg and when she walked out of the rehabilitation hospital. And he had been by her side ever since.

Jessica, on the other hand, was there for the first week, then off and on during the next few, citing an enormous caseload. She was a public defender in the district attorney's office and often worked twelve and fourteen hours a day just to keep up. Even through the numbing pain and haze of painkillers, Tyler knew something wasn't right, but she attributed it to some sort of post-traumatic stress disorder. She was the one seriously injured, while Jessica hadn't even been knocked off her feet. She had seen Tyler lying in the ditch, bloody and unconscious, her leg a mangled mess. Jessica had called 911 and used a makeshift tourniquet to stop the blood gushing from her knee from draining her. Who wouldn't have some kind of reaction to all that?

But that wasn't it. Sure, they hadn't made the "in sickness and in health" commitment, but they were together; they were a couple, for crying out loud. They had shared the flu, food poisoning, cramps, and a bad case of poison ivy. They were supposed to be there for each other.

After Tyler's head cleared she began to see that when Jessica was there, she wasn't really there. When they were together, Jessica chattered about her cases, their friends, or anything else she could think of so as not to have to talk about the accident. When Tyler tried to bring it up, Jessica either shut down or made some feeble excuse to have to leave. They had used to sit on the couch together holding hands and watching TV or just watching the fire crackle in the hearth. Tyler had to ask Jessica to sit with her, and when she did accept, she always chose the side with her complete leg. She apparently thought if she got too close she'd catch something—or lose something. Then came Jessica's declaration.

It was a cold, rainy Sunday afternoon in the city. Tyler had been home for three months and was sitting on the couch drinking a cup of tea. Jessica was in the loveseat, her briefcase open, stacks of files on the table in front of her.

"You don't touch me anymore," Tyler said quietly. Jessica had come over to her place Saturday morning, as she had the previous two weekends, but other than an almost-perfunctory kiss on the cheek hadn't touched her or slept in her bed.

"I beg your pardon?" Jessica asked.

Jessica might have been able to conceal her emotions as a successful attorney, but Tyler knew how to read her subtle clues. The page Tyler had just turned introduced an entirely new chapter in their relationship.

"You haven't touched me since the accident."

Jessica frowned, her eyes darting from Tyler to the file in her lap. "What are you talking about? Of course I have."

Tyler could see Jessica breathing faster, a sure sign she was nervous.

"Other than kissing me on the cheek, and pretty quickly at that, when have you touched me?" Tyler didn't like the sound of her voice. It was too calm. She watched Jessica search for something to say. Tyler's heart started to hurt, and the feeling in the pit of her stomach told her everything she needed to know. She must have been a glutton for punishment because she had to hear Jessica say it.

"Why do you sleep in the guest room?"

"I told you, I don't want to accidently bump into you in the middle of the night. I don't want to hurt you." She had used the same excuse each of the nights they'd been together.

"It doesn't hurt anymore." She was lying, it hurt all the time, and the phantom pain was excruciating, but that was not the point of this conversation. "What does hurt is the fact that you can't stand to be near me."

"That's not true," Jessica said in her defense, a little too quickly.

"Let's not quibble with semantics, Jessica. You can out-argue me all day. You have not touched me in any way other than platonically since the accident. Paul is more affectionate and he never claimed to be in love with me." Tyler's hands started to shake and she wanted to throw up, but she took a few deep breaths. She had to get to the bottom of this. It wasn't in her nature to let things simmer.

Jessica wouldn't look at her and she pressed on. "Do you still love me? I'm still the same person I was before the accident. Have I changed to the point that…" Tyler stopped, the complete truth hitting her like a stone. How silly of her to think she was the same person. She wasn't. She was missing half her leg, had months of physical and occupational therapy in front of her, and probably would never walk without a limp. But that wasn't what Jessica had fallen in love with, was it? By the look of absolute terror on Jessica's face, Tyler saw she was right.

"I'm sorry, Tyler." Jessica said. "I, we, I…" Tyler watched as Jessica struggled to find the words. She didn't intend to give her an easy escape so she kept quiet.

"When we go out, people stare at us. They look at you and then at me with pity in their eyes and I—" This time Tyler couldn't hold her tongue.

"For God's sake, Jessica, this isn't about you. *I* lost my leg, not you. My life will *never* be the same. I'll always have to use a cane or a crutch or a goddamn fake leg just to get to the bathroom, for Christ sake. And you're worried about what people are thinking about *you*?"

"I can't help it," she said angrily, tossing files into her briefcase. "Maybe I'm selfish, maybe I just don't have the Nurse Barton gene, but I can't do this. I look at you and see what we used to do together—run, swim, rock climb—and I…I look at your leg and…" Jessica stopped.

"And?" Tyler prompted her, even though she really didn't want to know the answer.

"I can't. It's all red and swollen and ugly, and watching it move is just freaky. And the thought of it wrapped around me like you used to…" She didn't finish her sentence, instead snapped her briefcase closed. "I'm sorry, Tyler. I thought I could do this, but I can't."

Tyler watched Jessica walk across the room and out of her life. She never heard from her again. And now almost four years later, here was Paul not even hesitating to help.

"I'd appreciate it. Thanks, Paul. The sand is so fine it somehow crawled up my leg. I think it's going to be a problem." Tyler pulled her pant leg up above her knee.

She depressed a button and heard the familiar click that released the lock in the bottom of the socket of the prosthesis. Paul watched as she pulled her stump out of the opening.

"Can you hold Lucy?" she asked, handing him the prosthesis.

Paul laughed, brushing his blond hair out of his eyes. "I still can't believe you named your leg. Is that common?"

"I don't know," Tyler replied, stripping off the sock and peeling the suction liner down until it too was off. "Whether or not I like it, it's a part of me and seems a little less machine-like with a name like Lucy. Francis Fibia just doesn't have the same ring."

"Ya think?" Paul shook his head.

Tyler brushed the sand off her thigh as best as she could. "This is only the beginning. If I can't keep the sand out of this it'll rub my stump raw. Then I'll really have a problem." One of the first things they drilled into her in rehab was to keep her stump healthy and her prosthesis clean. If she couldn't wear it, her mobility would be severely limited. And she wasn't about to have to rely on anyone in this group to help her. Other than Paul, of course.

"You know you can count on me," Paul said, flashing one of his charismatic smiles with not an ounce of pity evident.

"That's why I brought you along on this trip. What a fiasco." Tyler repeated her earlier actions and secured the prosthesis. When she heard the final click, Paul offered her a hand and she stood, testing the fit. She rolled her pants down. "Okay, Davey Crockett, let's go exploring."

❖

As Kristin watched them walk away, panic threatened to overwhelm her. Tyler and Paul were the only people who seemed to know what to do in this terrible situation. What would the rest of them do if something happened? Looking around her at their current surroundings she had flashes of what that something would be. If they weren't on the island alone, the other inhabitants might rescue them, but if they were the unsavory sort, her group might be in a worse position. Would wild animals attack rather than avoid them?

Kristin shook her head to stop the doomsday thoughts that threatened to overwhelm her. They wouldn't do any good. Abruptly she stood up. What would Blake do? She might not know, but she had read all of Blake Hudson's adventures and she'd been in this situation before. Well, maybe not this exact situation, but something similar.

What would Tyler do? What would Blake do? In her mind she saw that Tyler was Blake or vice versa. When Kristin thought of one she often thought of the other, they were that intertwined. Both were strong, both calm in a crisis, and both didn't take shit from anyone. She was once like that.

Kristin looked around. How in the hell had she gotten herself into this situation? She had an MBA from Sloan and here she was stranded on an island with a bunch of almost-total strangers and a man she barely knew anymore. How did she let this happen? She had done everything expected of her and more. Yet somehow it all just slipped away.

"Kristin, are you daydreaming again?" Steven's voice, once so quiet and soothing, now always sounded gruff and demanding. She used to love his slight British accent. It used to be sexy. Now she immediately stiffened when she heard it.

"Kristin," he barked again when she didn't respond fast enough.

"No, Steven, just thinking about what we should be doing."

"We should be watching for a rescue ship or plane."

"And why are we supposed to be doing that?" she replied, uncharacteristically questioning him. "No one knows we're even missing. No one is expecting us on the island, and everyone at home knows we're out of touch for five days."

"Are you saying this is my fault?" he asked in that familiar ugly tone.

"Of course not," she lied. It *was* his fault. He insisted on this ridiculous notion of total-incommunicado nonsense. For God's sake he was the CEO of a major corporation and this was most of his senior staff. How could they be completely out of touch? Only an egomaniac would consider that an okay thing to do. She thought about changing her tone to be more compliant, then changed her mind. "I'm just stating the obvious."

"If it's so obvious then why are you even mentioning it at all?"

Kristin knew she was in a no-win position. But when was the last time they had a normal, regular conversation? Steven usually ordered and those around him jumped.

Kristin struggled to remember what she had been thinking just moments ago. More often than not lately she simply slipped away in her mind to survive. It wasn't right, life should be much more than this, but she couldn't find the strength to do anything about it.

"We'd better get ready, it'll be dark soon," she said. She walked away from Steven, leaving him grumbling about something she more than likely didn't want to hear.

❖

"How much farther do you want to go?"

Tyler stopped, put her hands on her hips, and looked around. The landscape hadn't changed in the last half hour and, if anything, had only gotten more desolate. The trees were thinner and farther from the shore. The waves crashed over rocks on the beach, and cliffs towered off to their right.

"I guess we should head back. It's pretty obvious there's nothing this way." Tyler put her hand over her eyes, shading them from the afternoon sun. A bird squawked behind them and Paul jumped.

"Jeez, that scared the shit out of me." Paul patted his chest, mimicking the beating of his heart.

Tyler couldn't help but laugh. "God, Paul, you're such a queen. We're in the middle of nowhere. What did you expect?

"The honking of a taxi would be more to my liking."

"Well, you'd better get used to it and a whole lot more."

"You mean like lions, and tigers, and bears?" he asked, feigning fright. Paul was a huge fan of the movie *The Wizard of Oz* and used that phrase frequently when describing the unknown.

"Something like that, Dorothy, because we sure as hell aren't in Kansas anymore." Tyler laughed for the first time all day.

Kristin saw them first, two small dots down the beach. She had worried when they left and kept a watchful eye out the entire time.

As they got nearer she saw that Tyler was limping badly, holding on to Paul's arm for support. A pang of sympathy went through her heart for whatever was causing her pain. Tyler must have seen her because a moment later her limp became less noticeable, even though she still held Paul's arm.

"Did you find anything? What did you see? Where are we?" The choir of questions greeted Tyler and Paul when they returned. Kristin didn't know Tyler very well, but could see the edge of pain in her eyes. She brought both of them a bottle of water, cracking open the lid for Tyler and handing it to her.

"Thanks," Tyler replied, her voice tight. She took only two swallows before putting the cap back on.

"You need more than that," Kristin said. The last thing they needed was for Tyler to collapse due to dehydration. Out of all of them, she seemed to be the only one with any idea what to do. Tyler looked at her and Kristin felt something deep inside shift. Tyler's eyes were mysterious and she wanted to know what was behind them. "You need to stay hydrated," she added, feeling stupid for stating the obvious. Unlike Steven, who would have said something snarky, Tyler didn't, just took another couple of swallows.

"We walked about an hour, which was probably about two or three miles. It's more of the same as here," Tyler said. "Lots of rock, a few trees, and a lot of shoreline. We saw some fruit and berries, but that was about it. Tomorrow we'll go that way." She pointed in the opposite direction. "Maybe we'll find something else. In the meantime, we should probably settle in. It'll be dark soon, and we should gather as much wood as we can and start a signal fire. We need to set up shifts to keep it going and keep watch."

Tyler looked at Steven, fully expecting him to object or make some other egotistical or asinine comments. When none came she said, "I'll take the first watch, followed by Paul. With so many of us we all should be able to get a full night's sleep." The men groaned.

"Do you mean we have to sleep out here?" Joan asked, complete revulsion on her perfectly smooth face. Her salon-coiffed hair was a mess and a smudge of mascara marred her left cheek.

Tyler sighed. If she had a dollar for the number of times already she'd asked herself how she'd gotten into this situation, she could hire a private helicopter to rescue them.

"Well, no, not if you don't want to. Sleep, that is," she said. "I'm sure someone would gladly give you their shift on the signal fire so they could sleep." Tyler was being intentionally provocative, already tired of the constant whining. And her leg hurt.

"I never—" Joan said in her most offended voice.

"My wife will not stand guard." Robert was so pompous he was comical. His swollen nose didn't make him any more serious either.

"I don't care if she sits, stands, or jumps rope. Just so she doesn't let the fire go out. But if you'd like to take her shift in addition to your own, go right ahead." Tyler stared at each of the people in front of her for any other comments or arguments. Before anyone had a chance to say anything, she spoke again.

"We'll need a lot of wood to keep the fire going. There's driftwood all along the shoreline back there." Tyler indicated the direction she and Paul had come from. "If we all grab an armful or two we should have enough for the night. We can use the palm fronds to make smoke during the day if we see a boat or plane."

When only Kristin and Paul followed her, she said to no one in particular, "Come on, no one's going to get it for you."

"Who made you the boss?" Robert asked rudely from behind them. God, she hated him, Kristin thought. She normally didn't have such negative thoughts about people, but why couldn't he have broken his jaw instead of his nose? Then maybe he'd shut up. He'd always been a naysayer and had bitched the entire time Tyler and Paul were gone. Kristin didn't think anyone noticed, but Tyler cocked her head a fraction.

"Do you have a better idea?" she asked calmly. Kristin suspected she was anything but.

"You seem to have just come in and taken charge, telling everybody what to do. You're not even one of us." Robert looked first at Steven, then Mark for affirmation. He avoided eye contact with Paul altogether.

Tyler didn't seem rattled by Robert's outburst but simply replied, "You're right, Robert. I'm not a member of your little fraternity. I'm someone who, if I guess right, knows a little more about surviving in this situation than the rest of you. And I don't need to wait for someone else to grow some balls and take charge. So you and your little committee," Tyler hesitated, looking at Steven and Mark, "can do whatever you want, but I'm going to get what Paul and I need for the night."

Kristin watched the scene unfold in front of her. Robert always acted so high-and-mighty. She suspected that because he held the second-highest position at PPH, he believed he could say anything to anyone. She'd heard him talk down to people and be patronizing on more than one occasion. He'd tried it with Tyler the first time they met and she'd put him in his place. If he was arrogant enough to try it again with Tyler, Kristin suspected she'd nail him every time. Tyler had confidence without the familiar air of superiority Steven exuded. She didn't need to show off or throw her weight around to prove it. She was sexy.

Kristin inhaled sharply, glancing around to see if anyone noticed. She was shocked at the direction her thoughts had taken. They were stranded on an island, with no rescue in sight, and she was thinking Tyler was sexy. What had gotten into her? She must have hit her head harder than she thought.

CHAPTER NINE

Where's the rest of it?"
Tyler bit her tongue to keep from replying in the same arrogant, demanding tone that Joan had used since they arrived on the island.

"That's all you get for tonight."

"What do you mean, that's all?" Joan spat her reply, her harsh Boston accent thick. "I know for a fact that a hell of a lot more food than this came out of that airplane." She used the granola bar in her hand like a pointer directed at Paul. "I saw you bring it back."

Several of the others nodded their agreement, along with a few murmurs of support. The thick humidity in the night air added to the growing tension. Tyler had just given everyone their "dinner." "We talked about how we need to ration our supplies."

"*We* didn't talk about anything," Joan replied, her brash bottle-red hair blowing in all directions. "You told us what we were going to do. I don't think anyone voted on it."

Tyler looked around and all eyes were on her. Her fellow passengers except Kristin and Paul resembled a pack of hyenas licking their chops, knowing that one of them wouldn't come out of this unscathed. Kristin looked more scared than anticipatory and Paul, her dear friend Paul. He knew more about her than anyone, especially that she was the type to kick ass and not even bother to take names. His expression said these people had absolutely no idea who they thought they could bully.

"You're right, Joan, we didn't vote on it." Tyler did her best to appear calm and keep her voice steady. "But we don't know how long we'll be here. We have to plan for the worst, which includes rationing what little edible food we have. It's not like we can run down to the corner market to pick up a few things." She suspected none of these ladies did their household's weekly shopping.

"Where's the rest of it?" Robert asked, supporting his wife. His pale skin already showed signs of sunburn.

Tyler pointed to the pile with the rest of the supplies and items they'd salvaged from the plane. "Over there. But let me ask you something. All of you," she said, moving her hand around the semicircle where they'd gathered for their meal.

"When was the last time any of you did more than open the pantry or refrigerator or make reservations for dinner? And I don't mean deep-sea fishing off the stern of a forty-foot chartered boat complete with a fish finder?" She knew no one would answer and she wasn't wrong.

"Any of you see the movie *Castaway* with Tom Hanks?" Several heads grudgingly nodded. "Remember the scene after the crash and he was trying to catch a fish?" A few more nods. "Well, ladies and gentlemen, that is us. So unless any of you have some hidden talent in that area, or some other magical powers that can zap us up some food, we need to eat only what we need to survive. Not what we want, but what we need."

"You can't keep us from taking it. There's seven of us and only one of you." Steven spoke this time.

This is ridiculous, Tyler thought. They sounded more like children than grown men.

"Six," Paul said.

"I knew you'd side with her," Robert said from her left. "She's your girlfriend."

"I don't care if she's Attila the Hun," Paul replied. "Tyler knows more about what to do in this type of situation than all of us put together could even imagine. I'm just as hungry as you are, but think about it. If we eat everything tonight, what are we going to do for breakfast? And lunch and dinner tomorrow, and the next day, and the day after that?"

Mark replied confidently. "Someone will rescue us by then."

"And what if they don't?" Paul said quietly. Clearly the two men weren't used to backing down or losing. "Come on, guys, look at the facts," Paul said. "We crashed in God knows where. We haven't seen a plane or ship all day and it's too dark for any kind of search-and-rescue now, so we're here for the night. Let's concentrate on getting through that, and when the sun comes up we'll work on getting through tomorrow."

Even though it wasn't her style, Tyler could appreciate Paul's finesse with his peers. She would have simply said tough shit and dealt with the consequences, but she had to admit Paul's approach was working. Robert took Joan's arm and with a backward glance over his shoulder glared at Tyler before walking away, followed by Mark and Patty. Kristin stayed behind with Steven.

"I didn't need your help," Tyler said to Paul as they left the group.

"I wasn't helping you, I was helping me," he answered, ripping open his granola bar. "Sit down and eat." He dropped to the sand.

Tyler followed his example and sat, albeit more carefully than Paul. "And how is that?"

"It's like this," he said, stopping to take a bite of his dinner. "I am definitely not the Tom Hanks type. Never was, never will be, and don't want to be. However, he is kinda cute. If they eat all the food," he took another bite of his bar, "well, let's just say I promise you, Tyler, I'll starve to death if you don't take care of me."

Tyler couldn't help but laugh and shake her head. "I can always count on you to see the practical side of things, Paul. Always looking out for number one, as usual." Paul rarely thought of anyone other than himself and his needs, except for her. She loved him in spite of it and because of it at the same time.

"You'd better open that and eat it before I knock you on the head, take it from you, and blame Robert. You know I can do it."

"After that butch little scene I'm scared of you, big guy," Tyler replied.

Kristin watched Tyler slowly and methodically open her granola bar. She started at one end and gently pulled the wrapping apart, careful not to tear it. Once it was open she slowly separated the seam down the middle of the wrapping, repeating the same careful movements on the opposite end. She seemed to be using every movement of opening the small bar as part of the meal. When it was completely open she pressed the paper flat, put her hands in her lap, and lowered her head.

Was she praying? Tyler didn't move for several seconds. Kristin didn't move either until Tyler took a small bite. When she deeply exhaled, Kristin realized she'd been holding her breath.

It felt like she'd held it during the entire ugly episode with Joan Brown. God, that woman was selfish. In the years that Kristin had known her she had concluded that Joan believed that a woman couldn't be too rich, too thin, too redheaded, or too self-centered.

And the others. How quick they were to gang up on Tyler. They were like a pack of dogs, waiting to follow their alpha. Why couldn't they see Tyler was trying to help all of them, even the ones that didn't deserve it?

Kristin admired the way Tyler had handled herself. She didn't get ruffled or stammer like she would have. Kristin hated herself when her mind went completely blank. She felt like a fool. Tyler stayed cool, recited the facts, and easily deflected anything thrown at her. At least it appeared that it was easy for her. She knew Tyler to be quick with a comeback, say the right words, and never appeared to let anyone or anything intimidate her. Kristin really admired the way Tyler had reacted and handled herself in the past twelve hours.

Tyler seemed to thrive in this situation. She appeared more confident than when they had been together before, more sure of herself, if that was possible. She hadn't been a wallflower in other social situations, but out here in nature she seemed more at home.

Kristin remembered when she felt the same. Before she married Steven she loved working outdoors alongside her father on the job site. She loved the smell of cut plywood and two-by-four pine studs. The sound of electric saws, nail guns, and old-fashioned hammers methodically nailing solid pieces of wood together was more comfortable than the clinking of crystal champagne glasses at a fine restaurant. She missed it. She felt more comfortable on the job site than in an office, at least when she had an office. Her mother had a picture of her wearing a tool belt and hard hat, standing next to her father. Both were ten times too big for her, for she was only three years old. She still had that tool belt in a box tucked away in another box in the attic. Steven had told her to get rid of it years ago, but she never did. She couldn't.

Kristin watched Tyler savor every bite and chew as if it were her last. Who knows, without her knowledge and outright command of their situation it could very well have been her last. The thought frightened Kristin. What would they do tomorrow? And the next day and the next, as Paul had so clearly outlined. Their meager food supply would run out sooner rather than later, and she didn't trust Steven's staff not to take more than their fair share. Joan had practically accused Tyler of hiding some of it.

"I'm still hungry."

Steven's voice startled her. She was so deep in thought she'd forgotten he was sitting beside her. "I know, try not to think about it."

"How am I supposed to not think about it?" He scoffed. "The more you try not to think about something, the more you do." He angrily tossed the empty wrapper in front of her. "This isn't enough to keep a bird alive, let alone a grown man."

Kristin took another bite of her dinner, mimicking Tyler's movements. She wasn't sure when she had started, but watching her, doing what she did seemed to soothe her fears.

"Get me another one," Steven said.

Kristin dragged her eyes away from Tyler. "What?"

"You heard me, get me another one. I'm starving. I haven't had anything to eat all day."

Steven was exaggerating. They'd had a similar meal earlier that afternoon. "Steven, you heard what Tyler said."

"I don't give a shit what she said. Nobody put her in charge. I'm the CEO of this company and what I say goes."

Kristin wished she had a dollar for every time she'd heard that line. She had long ago decided that any man who had to say it ruled with threats and power, not influence or respect. "No, Steven, no one put her in charge, but you have to admit she seems to know what she's doing, what we need to be doing. Besides, Steven, you can't do much." She indicated his broken leg, now splinted, thanks to Tyler, in tree branches, wrapped in cloth torn from something they had recovered from the plane. She didn't even try to sound appeasing.

"I've got a broken leg, not a limp dick. Now get me something else to eat. Something substantial, not that sissy granola bar."

"Here, take the rest of mine." Kristin had a PowerBar, which seemed to satisfy him, for the time being anyway. She knew it wouldn't last.

CHAPTER TEN

The stars were brighter than Kristin had ever seen them. She glanced at her watch and was surprised when the glowing hands on the face indicated only nine thirty. She was exhausted. Her body felt like it was closer to midnight than two hours since sundown.

Steven had barked orders at her and the others, and their camp looked nothing like Tyler's. Even though Tyler had only taken a few things from the communal supply area, her and Paul's canopy was tight, angled away from their sleeping area, their signal fire burning brightly. Theirs, on the other hand, was billowing in the stiff breeze, and Robert had yet to get their fire started.

Kristin cringed as Steven snarled at her yet again. She knew he was in pain and had never been a good patient even under the best circumstances, but he had been particularly nasty this entire trip.

"What are you doing?"

"I'm resting a minute." She'd been hauling and stacking driftwood near their yet-unlit fire. She went to the gym four times a week, but nothing could have prepared her for the physical exertion of the last hour.

"We don't have time to take a break. Do you think the weather will wait for you to get everything done? This tarp needs to come over another few feet. I don't want to get wet if it rains."

Kristin tuned him out and turned to gather more firewood, but Tyler drew her attention. She stood next to Paul by their fire, her back to Kristin and the others. She and Paul had offered to help, but Steven had declined decisively. He hadn't waited until they were out of earshot before adding something derogatory about their obvious switch in gender roles. Kristin saw Paul keep Tyler from turning around and saying something. Kristin wondered what she would have said if he hadn't.

Tyler looked tall and powerful in the glow of the fire. The shadow cast a silhouette that emphasized her lean, muscular form, and Kristin's heart beat faster. She looked exactly like Kristin's mental image of Blake Hudson. With every Expedition book, Tyler had made Blake come alive. She was strong, fearless, confident, and always in control. What she couldn't accomplish physically, she used her brain and ingenuity to figure out. In Kristin's mind she was a combination of beauty and brains. Looking at Tyler, she thought the same thing.

She wondered about Tyler's life, what she had experienced that shaped the woman she was today. Did she have a happy childhood, great parents, and lots of friends? What was her favorite subject in school, her favorite color? Did she like pizza and beer or filet and shrimp?

Tyler turned and Kristin felt her eyes on her and blushed, thinking that Tyler had read her thoughts. Tyler couldn't possibly know what she'd been thinking, but she felt exposed nonetheless. This time her pulse raced when Tyler walked toward her.

"There's no need to have two signal fires. We'll just waste good wood. We'll keep ours lit." Tyler stood to her left, glancing at their pile of logs.

"I'm sorry," Kristin said quietly moving closer to their yet-unlit fire so Steven couldn't hear.

Tyler turned her attention back to her. "For what?"

Kristin lifted her hands and shrugged.

"No apologies necessary. We're in a tough spot here. Tempers are bound to be short. It's important that we stick together and work together."

"Together-we-stand, divided-we-fall kind of thing?" Kristin gave a smile, rewarded with Tyler's in return.

"Something like that, yeah."

Kristin watched Tyler's chest rise and fall and realized she was matching her breath for breath. She had to stop. She was married to Steven and, for God's sake, Tyler was with Paul. The love between them was obvious. They didn't act like any other couple she knew. They had a rare connection almost palpable, yet elusive at the same time. Kristin had no doubt they loved each other. They were demonstrative without being inappropriate, and each seemed to know where the other was even if they were out of eyesight of each other.

"I'm glad you're here," Kristin said, and saw Tyler's bemused expression.

"We'd probably still be sitting in our seats waiting for the coast guard to show up in their shiny red-and-white boats, flaunting their buff bodies and regulation haircuts."

"I think they're orange-and-white, and while I prefer curves to buff, right now I'd be happy to see Tarzan swing from one of those trees." Tyler used her thumb to indicate the ones behind them.

"That would certainly generate some interesting conversation. Joan would probably faint over his choice of clothing designers." Kristin mumbled under her breath but, judging by Tyler's chuckle, not quietly enough.

Several minutes passed with no conversation. If not for their situation, the waves lapping on the shore would be soothing and tranquil.

"I suppose you organized things while we were gone."

It sounded to Kristin more like a comment than a question. 'Yeah, well, someone needed to do it," she answered, oddly warmed. A natural organizer, Kristin had made some sense of the items they'd recovered from the plane. She'd arranged suitcases by owner, placed food on faux shelves she created out of driftwood and stones, and piled blankets and pillows neatly on a larger boulder. Backpack and briefcases were slightly away from the other luggage. Some of it had been soaking wet, though almost everything had dried under the sun's heat.

Tyler stood beside her silently for some time. Kristin didn't want the conversation to end so she said, "How's your leg?" She felt, more than saw, Tyler stiffen beside her.

"Fine." Tyler replied in a tone Kristin interpreted as I-don't-want-to-talk-about-it.

"It's none of my business but you seemed to be limping more than usual." Kristin cringed at her choice of words. She'd told Tyler that she'd noticed her limp before. How insensitive.

"It's fine. You okay?" Tyler asked, turning the tables on her.

"Yeah, thanks." Kristin lied. She was anything but okay. She was hungry, frightened, and confused over her sudden feelings toward Tyler.

"Where do you think we are?"

Tyler turned to Kristin. She had absolutely no clue but didn't think it would do either of them any good to voice her fear. "Somewhere near where we were headed, I hope."

Kristin gathered her hair in her hand and secured it with a large clip. "Steven said he was having a problem with the instruments before the hydraulics went out."

"Did he get a Mayday out?" Tyler asked, looking back to the horizon. She knew enough about flying to realize that they certainly taught the universal distress code in flying school.

"No." Kristin answered so quietly Tyler almost didn't hear her.

"No?"

Kristin shook her head.

"Well, the people on the island will call the authorities when we don't arrive. We just have to sit tight till they find us." When Kristin didn't immediately reply she turned to fully look at her.

"Tell me." Tyler rarely panicked, preferring to deal with the facts as she knew them. This, however, was an entirely different situation.

"No one is expecting us."

Kristin's face conveyed that she was afraid to say anymore. Tyler prompted her.

"What do you mean no one is expecting us? There are workers on the island." She stopped when Kristin shook her head. "Household help?" Again a negative reply. "No one is on the island?" This time Kristin didn't bother to answer.

"Great, this just keeps getting better." Tyler rubbed her thigh. Between the crash, walking on the sand, and getting the camp set up, her leg was killing her. Her pain pills had survived being submerged in the water, but she didn't want to take one unless it was absolutely necessary. Who knew how long it would be until they were rescued.

"Who else knows this?"

"Nobody." Kristin didn't add anything else.

"Why are you telling me?" Tyler felt the heat from Kristin standing next to her, their shoulders almost touching.

"Because you and Paul are the only ones actually *doing* anything. Everybody else is sitting on their ass waiting for a helicopter to drop out of the sky and rescue us. Talk about a fantasy."

Just then Steven called for her, his voice booming in the quiet night. "Kristin. Go help Mark. That stupid bean counter can't do anything without his calculator."

The look of apology and embarrassment on Kristin's face tore at Tyler's heart. She repeated her earlier question. "Are you okay?" She didn't expect Kristin to answer anything other than yes. She had too much pride. When Kristin said yes and turned to walk away, Tyler did as well. For some odd reason she didn't want to see her leave.

❖

"How are you doing?" Paul asked when Tyler returned to their fire. He helped her sit down.

"As best as can be expected. How about you, my I-don't-like-to-get-my-hands-dirty-gay-BFF?" She nudged him with her shoulder.

"You know me too well, my little I'll-never-admit-I'm-in-pain-butch-BFF." He nudged her back. After a quiet moment he said, "What a nice mess you've gotten me into, Ollie," mimicking one of the famous lines in a Laurel and Hardy movie.

"Me? I was just supposed to be the eye candy, and here I am being Tarzan to your Jane." Paul laughed, and Tyler with him.

"Very good comeback. That sounds like something Blake would say. Now tell me how you really are."

Tyler rubbed her leg. "I'm scared."

"Me too."

"And I'm trying not to show it."

"Me too."

"And I just want to get off this island, back on solid ground, and have a cold beer or two, maybe even three or four."

"Me too."

"And I want to kiss Kristin Walker."

"Got me on that one."

"Actually I want to do more than kiss your boss's wife."

This time he didn't reply.

"Is that crazy or what? I mean, look at us. We've crashed-landed in God-only-knows-where, we're sitting in front of a signal fire, no idea when we'll be rescued because nobody even knows we're missing, and all I can think about is untying that little rope belt on Kristin's pants." She certainly thought it odd. This wasn't real. She should be scared to death, worried about what they'd have for breakfast other than the bags of peanuts they'd retrieved from the galley, not wondering how soft the skin was underneath Kristin's shirt.

"Not really. People handle stress in weird ways."

Tyler bumped him again. "By thinking about boffing the boss's wife? Get real, Paul. Even that's out there."

"No, really. I read an article once about how stress can make everything more intense. You're more in tune with your surroundings, your senses are heightened. All the superfluous stuff just goes away. Kind of like survival of the fittest."

"Food, fresh water, and shelter are superfluous?"

"No, you're not getting it. Let me spell it out for you."

Paul stopped and Tyler said, "Please. My head hurts, my stomach's growling, and I want a hot shower. I'm not following."

"Listen closely and learn, butterfly," Paul said in a fake Kung Fu voice. "When people are thrown together in a life-or-death situation they have a basic primal need to survive. Connecting with someone, especially sexually, is basic survival." Paul stoked the fire.

"Is that it?" Tyler asked, expecting more.

"Yep."

"And who discovered that?"

"I don't know, Freud or somebody."

"I doubt it was Freud. But I'd bet a man came up with that one. How convenient."

Paul teased her. "Well, we are the smarter gender."

"You're a big help. Don't give up your day job and become a sex therapist. Oh, on second thought you might not have a day job to go back to if I don't keep my mouth shut around your boss. And my hands off his wife," she muttered.

"What did you say now?" Paul groaned. Tyler always pushed the limits of putting her foot in her mouth but never while she was his "girlfriend."

"They started it." Tyler felt Paul's shoulder shake while he snickered.

"Spoken like a true leader. Don't fret about it, darling. We have more than that to worry about. Now tell me about your lust for my boss's wife. I'm practically worthless out here in nature, but that I can help you with." Paul leaned back on his arms, fully expecting her to tell him.

She couldn't talk about it, at least not yet. She wasn't sure herself what it was. Every time Steven raised his voice to Kristin or spoke to her with no respect, she almost got in his face and screamed at him. Better yet, she felt like rescuing Kristin and treating her like she deserved to be treated. But what was she thinking? Kristin was a grown woman, married for many years and perfectly capable of taking care of herself. If Kristin allowed herself to be treated like this then who was she to say it wasn't right? Just because she wouldn't say anything other than kind words to her was another matter altogether. If Kristin wanted out of her marriage, then surely she would go. Wouldn't she?

"Don't you think it's not real smart to have almost your entire senior leadership team on the same flight?" Tyler asked instead. She needed to deflect the subject away from her confusing feelings about Kristin. She couldn't deal with them right now.

"What?" Paul asked, obviously confused by the quick change of topic.

"I mean, come on. What CEO would put all his eggs in one basket like Walker did? If the plane went down, like it did, I might add, who's left to run the company?"

"Who cares? Everybody would be dead."

"Probably, but still. Who's running the joint now?" Tyler asked, realizing she had no idea and hadn't thought of it before.

"No one. We're shut down for the week. It's our annual holiday. Everyone's out." Paul tossed a twig into the fire. It flared then died down. "You're avoiding the subject."

"No, I'm not."

"You've never been attracted to a straight woman, have you?" Paul never gave up.

"No. Straight women, no matter how hot, just don't turn me on."

"But Kristin does?"

"I don't want to talk about it." It was going to be a battle to see who won this conversation, and she was tired from fighting the urge to take Kristin in her arms and kiss her when they were standing next to each other earlier.

"You never answered my question on the plane."

"What question?"

"When was the last time you asked a woman out just for dinner? And not used it as foreplay? A year? Two? Three?"

Each year that Paul counted, Tyler's nerves became more jagged. The truth hurts when it hits home, she thought. "I don't kiss and tell."

"No, but you do fuck, and you don't tell about that either. When was the last time someone other than me saw you naked?"

"Paul," Tyler said, knowing what was coming next. Paul had been ragging her for months about her relationships with women. They weren't relationships by any stretch of the imagination. They were quick, sometimes anonymous, and always strictly physical. No one other than her doctors and Paul had seen her naked, to answer Paul's question. She wasn't self-conscious about her leg, often wearing shorts when the weather was nice. But to actually be in bed with a woman, making love, was still just a bit freaky, even to herself.

"You deserve better than that, Tyler."

"That's enough." She uncharacteristically snapped at Paul, then took a few deep breaths to calm down. What Paul had said was partially true. She'd been out on dates since the accident. More specifically, since Jessica abandoned her. Dozens, as a matter of fact. She'd taken beautiful women to dinner, the theater, and an occasional lunch in the park. She'd kissed them, gotten them naked, and made them come. But she hadn't exposed herself either physically or emotionally. She didn't know which scared her more.

"The women I'm with want the same thing I do, nothing more. Don't make it sound cheap or tawdry because it's not."

"No," Paul said quietly. "It's lonely."

Goddamn truth, she thought.

CHAPTER ELEVEN

S omeone screamed. Tyler sat upright, looking to her left. She wasn't asleep, hadn't been able to sleep thinking of Kristin lying not more than fifteen feet from her.

"What the hell?" someone asked. Everyone was now awake and looking around.

Tyler stumbled to her feet. She hadn't removed her prosthesis when she lay down for just this reason. If something happened in the night and she needed to move quickly, stopping to put her leg on could mean the difference between life and death.

Joan was staring into the darkness, Robert beside her. "What's the matter?" Tyler asked, hobbling over to her. No one, other than Paul and Kristin, had done more than sit up.

"I saw something move over there," she replied, pointing in the direction of the trees.

"What was it?" Tyler asked, squinting. As if that would enable her to see into the pitch-black jungle.

"I don't know. It looked like a pair of eyes, and the branches around it moved." She ended her sentence by burying her head into Robert's chest.

"Did you see anything?" Tyler asked him.

"No, I was looking in the other direction."

He was lying. Looking at the back of his closed eyelids was more like it.

"What should we do?" Kristin asked, over her right shoulder.

Tyler listened for any sound that might indicate they weren't alone on the beach. She soon gave up, knowing an animal would be far more experienced in stealth than she was in detecting it.

"Increase the people on watch to two. One facing the beach, the other the trees. That way we won't miss anything in either direction." She glanced at her watch. It was almost time for another shift.

"I have the next shift," Kristin said, as if reading her mind. Not surprisingly, nobody moved.

"I'll sit the watch with you," Tyler said.

"You just finished yours a few hours ago," Kristin said, and Tyler heard the concern in her voice.

"I don't see anyone else jumping up to protect the clan. That and the fact that I might as well, since I'm wide-awake now. She tossed another log on the fire, sparks drifting into the night sky.

"I'll get us a blanket," Kristin said, heading in the direction of where she'd been lying. In a minute she returned carrying a blue blanket that Tyler had seen her cover herself with earlier. The night air had become damp and cool.

They sat beside each other, facing opposite ways, the blanket over their legs. The large, soft blanket wasn't like any scratchy airplane blanket she'd ever used. Tyler didn't think that whatever Joan had seen earlier, if anything, would be back any time that night. If it did, it was probably just curious. In her research for Blake's adventures, Tyler had learned that most animals were more afraid of humans than vice versa. When they attacked they were usually protecting their young or feeling trapped.

Tyler watched Kristin sift sand through her fingers as the minutes ticked away. The silence between them was comforting yet begged to be filled. Tyler wanted to learn everything about the woman sitting beside her. But she couldn't. Shouldn't. Besides the fact that she was her BFF's boss's wife, the ring on Kristin's left hand was glittering in the firelight. She was somebody else's wife. Tyler had never cheated, had never been tempted, and had vowed never to be involved, however briefly, with someone who did. She had changed a lot since the accident but that part of her character never would.

"Why did you give Steven part of your dinner?" The question seemed to throw Kristin off because it took her a few beats to answer.

"I wasn't that hungry," she replied, looking away.

Tyler knew a bullshit answer when she heard one. "You need to eat, keep your strength up and your mind sharp."

"I said I wasn't hungry," Kristin replied, less convincingly this time.

"Everybody gets their share and you need to not share yours." Tyler knew she sounded stern, but it pissed her off that Steven was so demanding. Actually she didn't know if she was angry at Steven's behavior or at Kristin for putting up with it. If he were her husband, he...well, point in fact, someone like Steven would never be her husband in the first place.

The conversation died and Tyler tried not to stare as the light breeze blew Kristin's hair off her face. The fire crackled with life, and the still night air carried the sound of the waves crashing against the rocks a few hundred yards away.

Finally after what seemed like forever, Kristin asked, "Did you get any sleep?"

"No."

"Me either."

"What kept you awake?"

Kristin scanned the horizon in front of her. "You mean other than the obvious, or the fact that it's so quiet you can hear yourself think?"

That was an interesting choice of words, Tyler thought. She asked about it.

"You know, no distractions, nothing to hide behind."

Tyler's stomach clenched. She didn't want to get into a deep philosophical conversation with Kristin. She didn't want to know her thoughts, what she was afraid of hearing in the quiet. She couldn't seem to stop herself from asking anyway.

"What are you hiding from?"

"Myself."

It was such a simple reply, Tyler wasn't sure she heard it correctly. Why on earth would she be telling this to a near-stranger? Especially to her, the almost-wife of one of her husband's employees? Kristin was an amazingly beautiful woman. What had caused the sadness and defeat she heard in her voice?

Kristin brushed the sand from her hands as if wiping away her comment. She sat up straighter and Tyler could almost feel her regain control. "I'm sorry, that was terribly inappropriate. I hope I didn't embarrass you or make you feel uncomfortable."

"No, not at all. Sometimes it's easier to talk to a stranger than someone you know." She, however, never talked about anything important to anyone other than Paul.

"But you're not really a stranger. I've known you, what, about three or four years now?"

Tyler hadn't really kept track. "I wouldn't call seeing someone two or three times a year knowing them. Especially in the situations we find ourselves in. You're always the hostess with certain responsibilities, and I'm always the guest whose only job is to be polite and eat what's served." A warmth passed through Tyler at Kristin's quiet laugh.

"Guess you've got a point there. Wanna trade sometime?"

"Never." In more ways than one, Tyler thought.

"I do."

Here we go down that slippery slope again, Tyler thought. Time to put on the brakes. "Then why don't you?" Okay, obviously she needed new brakes.

"How come you and Paul aren't married?"

When Kristin asked the question it wasn't as intrusive as when Steven asked it. "Marriage, or what society defines as marriage, doesn't fit for what Paul and I have. We don't need to be married. We're committed to each other, and a ring and ceremony won't change that."

"I admire you," Kristin said, finally making eye contact. The fire danced on her face, casting shadows and accentuating her strong jawline. Tyler was mesmerized.

"You shouldn't. I'm not much different from everybody else." Especially every other lesbian on the face of the earth who would be equally thrilled to be sitting under the stars next to a woman as beautiful as Kristin.

"I beg to differ. You're a successful author, lead an exciting life, and have someone like Paul in love with you," Kristin said in all seriousness.

Tyler laughed quietly. "I'm not sure about the exciting life. I have a job just like everybody else, mine is just to write. What's a little different is the element of creativity in it that, if missing, seriously cuts into my work product," Tyler added trying to lighten the conversation. Thankfully, it worked.

"How did you get started writing?"

"Something to pass the time."

Kristin turned and looked at her. "I can't imagine you sitting around with nothing to do."

"Why do you say that?" Normally Tyler didn't care what people thought of her, but she wanted to know what Kristin did.

"I don't know. I guess because you're gorgeous and interesting. You probably had gobs of friends and men after you all the time. I just can't picture you sitting in front of the TV with the remote, flipping through the channels."

Tyler's pulse jumped when Kristin said she was gorgeous. Down, girl, she told herself. "Well, that's exactly what I would have been doing if I'd had a TV." Kristin was looking at her, expecting her to continue.

"I was working at Walmart, and after paying rent, my car payment, and a few groceries, there wasn't much left. I was never really interested in TV, other than reruns of *MacGyver*. I spent hours at the library instead." It didn't really bother her that she was the only one at school who didn't know the characters on the hottest shows in prime time. She'd eavesdrop on other conversations and then reiterate what she heard in other conversations. She wanted to fit in, but as much as she tried, she never really felt as though she did. Especially when she wanted to kiss Selena Duffy more than Rick Ward. So she would lose herself in books, stories of exciting people in exotic places doing fabulous things. Even as a teenager she loved to read books with strong female characters.

"So one day I just picked up a pen and a scrap of paper and started writing. The rest is history, as they say."

"Your parents must be very proud of you."

Tyler detected wistfulness in Kristin's tone but couldn't be sure. "That's an understatement. My dad's a bus driver for the city of Memphis and tells all his passengers about my latest book. My mom, who never read a book after graduating from high school, was the president of her local book club. She used to go around to the local Barnes & Noble bookstores to make sure they'd displayed my new release properly. My big brother teases me about being the famous author who flunked freshman English."

"You flunked freshman English?"

Tyler felt herself blush remembering how she could never quite make it to the eight a.m. class on Monday, Wednesday, and Friday because of Debra Parker. Kristin didn't need to know those details.

"Well, you know how it is when you're a freshman," Tyler said, letting Kristin's imagination fill in the rest.

"What was the first thing you wrote?" Thankfully Kristin changed the subject.

Even nineteen years later, Tyler could see the words as clearly as if they were in front of her. "The sun was just peeking over the horizon when she pulled out of the drive." Tyler would never forget them. They were the beginning of the rest of her life. Until the accident, that is. Then her definition of life completely changed.

"I don't remember any of your books starting like that."

Tyler shook her head, remembering her editor Roberta striking the entire first chapter. It was shocking at first, the number of changes that came back, but Roberta patiently explained the whys of her suggested changes, and Tyler learned about writing as a craft from every revision. "That's because that's the corniest, tritest way to begin a novel. I didn't know any better, but I do now."

"So where did Blake come from?"

"She developed over time. I had an image in my head of her character and she just morphed into it as I wrote."

"I envision her as a cross between Laura Croft from *Tomb Raider* and Audrey Hepburn."

"Really?" Tyler responded. Was it more than coincidence that was exactly how she saw her? Strong, yet elegant when she needed to be.

"I like her."

Tyler detected a little more than simple admiration in Kristin's voice. "Thanks, I'm kind of proud of her too."

"She's strong, not afraid to go after what she wants, and always knows exactly what to say."

"That's because she has several rewrites under her belt. When you have weeks to think about just the right thing to say, it usually comes out pretty good." That wasn't quite the truth. Tyler rarely had to rewrite her dialogue. She had what her editor called the gift of gab.

"Well, I think you're very talented. But you probably hear that all the time."

Tyler was used to accolades from book reviewers, the press, and individuals she met on the street or at book signings. But the sense of pride she felt from Kristin's simple compliment far exceeded any award or recognition she'd ever received.

"It still makes me feel good every time. We artistic types are very insecure, you know." Tyler's pulse beat faster when Kristin laughed. She had laughed more during this conversation than Tyler had heard her in the past few years. She was shocked when she realized she'd actually been counting.

"Yeah, right, and you toil away with your quill and parchment into the wee hours of the morning too, I suppose."

"Actually I do." When she was on a creative roll, she could write for hours without realizing the time, often skipping several meals before having to stop, usually due to exhaustion.

"Is that when you do your best work?"

Tyler coughed, choking on her own saliva with the X-rated image of Kristin that popped into her mind.

Kristin patted her on the back. "You okay?" she asked after several solid smacks.

"I am now. Something went down the wrong pipe, I guess." Tyler coughed a few more times, her eyes watering.

When she was finally able to speak she asked, "What do you like about Blake? Strictly research, of course." It always intrigued her that people connected with a character and always asked her fans all kinds of questions. Sometimes for research, sometimes for general conversation, but this time she really wanted to know what Kristin thought of her work.

"I don't know exactly. Like I said, she's tough, doesn't take any bullshit from anyone, and isn't afraid of anything. I guess I'd describe her as kind of butch, in a good way. I think she's sexy."

Tyler was speechless. Even though that's exactly the person Blake was in her mind, she certainly didn't expect to hear that descriptor coming from a straight woman, especially not from Kristin. After her conversation with Paul earlier in the day the thought that Kristin thought Blake sexy was interesting. Very interesting, and very dangerous.

"You must think this group is totally worthless," Kristin said, changing the subject and nodding in the direction of the sleeping figures.

"They are something, aren't they? I'd say more like helpless than worthless."

Kristin laughed. "You don't need to be PC with me. I think we're past that, don't you?"

Kristin stretched her arms out behind her on the sand and leaned back. A log in the fire cracked and a flame erupted, brightening her face. Tyler's mouth went dry and she could have sworn she stopped breathing. Kristin was the most beautiful woman she had ever seen, and she wanted her desperately.

"Whatever you say," she managed to croak out. The words had several different meanings, and Tyler meant every one of them. About now she'd do anything Kristin asked. And a few things she didn't.

CHAPTER TWELVE

The wind had died and it must have been low tide, because Tyler could barely hear even the sound of the waves. She lay on her back, hands folded under her head for her pillow. She hadn't slept much. When Mark and Patty relieved her and Kristin she said a quiet good night and lay down beside Paul. Judging by his snoring he wasn't having any trouble sleeping.

They had never been forced to share a room while on one of their charades so this trip was definitely a first. They very well couldn't ask for separate rooms if they were lovers. They had never given anyone the idea they were anything less than intimate, and she had added that item to her I-really-don't-want-to-do-this-trip list. It was directly below no-Internet-access and immediately above no-cable. She was a baseball junkie, with the uncanny ability to recite any stat on any player in any game she watched. Often she watched two games at the same time, courtesy of picture-within-a-picture on her sixty-two-inch Sony.

She used to play every Saturday and sometimes Sunday afternoon on a coed team, because their games were more interesting. But that was before the accident. Now she rarely went to the field—only when one of her friends dragged her along on their quest to snag the "cutie in right field" or "the hot shortstop." Someone else had taken her place as the hot shortstop, both literally and figuratively. Another adjustment in a long list of unplanned adjustments she had made in the past five years.

A comet streaked across the predawn sky like a firefly. One minute it was there, the next it was gone. How apropos, Tyler thought. Many elements of her life resembled that. One minute she was kissing Heather Wilson, the next having her face slapped. One minute she was stocking shelves at a Walmart, the next a best-selling author. One minute she was running along the side of a dirt road, the next lying alone in a hospital bed, her left leg amputated above the knee. How quickly things change.

Paul rolled over on his side, his snoring now little more than heavy breathing. His nose was perfect, he had cheekbones a model would kill for, and, unlike most men, had very little hair other than on his head. He worked hard to keep his body college-hard, as he called it. She loved him like no one she had ever loved. Sure, he was a guy and a gay guy on top of that, but he would still be her best friend even if he had married her sister.

Someone in their camp stirred, followed by a shadow passing in front of the fire. Tyler recognized the silhouette and watched as Kristin walked toward the water. Even in the soft sand, she moved with the grace of a dancer. Had she ever been one? She had long legs that, as her dad would say, ran from her ass all the way to the ground. Her hair blew in the light breeze, trailing behind her like a billowing curtain.

Why was she married to an ogre like Steven Walker, Tyler asked herself as she watched Kristin sit near the shore. She was beautiful, warm, a good conversationalist, and an absolute knockout. She could have any man she wanted. Did she forget to mention that she thought Kristin was drop-dead gorgeous? She had always found Kristin attractive, but something about their current situation had changed everything she thought and felt about her.

What was it? How did this happen? She had asked herself these questions several times during the night when sleep eluded her. She replayed practically every word of their conversation during their night watch. How ridiculous was that? She was thirty-nine years old, stranded on a desert island, and she was thinking like a teenager. God, this had the makings of a Harlequin romance, complete with the handsome hunk lying beside her. On the contrary, she might use this story line for her next Blake Hudson adventure.

Giving up on sleep, Tyler started to get up. Her leg was bothering her, the stump irritated due to sand, stress, and no telling what else. Even after all this time it throbbed if she wore the prosthesis too many hours without a break.

Stumbling awkwardly to her feet she followed Kristin's footprints toward the water. Her inner voice was telling her to go in the other direction, but she never listened to that voice unless she was writing. But this wasn't fiction. This was real.

"You're up early." The first rays of the morning trickled over Kristin's face as she turned and looked at her. Did she mention Kristin was stunningly beautiful?

"Ditto," Kristin replied.

"Yeah, well, I'm not real good sleeping someplace other than my own bed. May I join you?" As much as Kristin looked like she wanted to be alone, Tyler wanted to be with her more.

"Of course," she answered, patting the space beside her.

Tyler settled into the soft sand as gracefully as possible. Kristin obviously saw her awkwardness but didn't mention it. It was beginning to be the elephant in the very large room.

"You know, if we were here under any other circumstances, this would be quite a romantic scene." Kristin had turned her attention back to the sun now peeking from the horizon.

"Yes, it is," Tyler replied, surprised the words came out of her mouth so clearly. Her heart was pounding, her palms damp. An image of Kristin in her arms as they watched the sun rise and set flashed through her mind.

"I had a dream once that I was stranded on a desert island."

"Really?"

"It was years ago and, as a matter of fact, I used to have it often." Tyler encouraged her. "Tell me about it."

"I don't know what happened, how I got there, but I was alone. I climbed trees to get coconuts and bananas, somehow caught fish with a hook and a piece of rope that mysteriously washed ashore. I don't know how long I was there but I built a house, you know, like the Swiss Family Robinson." She stopped long enough for Tyler to nod her understanding. "I had tamed a wild pig and called it Sam. And, the funny thing is, I always had on the same clothes and they never wore out or got dirty."

Kristin finally smiled, which made the beams of the morning sun dim by comparison. "Well, it was a dream after all," Tyler said. "There's no sense being dirty and stinky in your own dream."

"This certainly isn't a dream."

The defeat in Kristin's voice shook Tyler. She wanted to hear the smile in her voice again. "It doesn't have to be a nightmare either. We just need to be smart and think about what we need to do, then do it. Today is one day closer to everyone realizing we're missing. One day closer to getting back to our homes, our friends, and our family. And a hot shower," Tyler added lightly.

A hot shower. That was exactly what Kristin wanted. She wasn't normally that hung up on being squeaky clean, preferring the mixture of sweat and dirt and hard work to expensive perfumes. But she felt grungy and sticky from the sweat and salt and knew she must smell like it too. But Tyler didn't seem to mind. She had sat down beside her and was still here.

"I'll take that and raise you a cup of coffee," she added, the sadness that had blanketed her for the past few months starting to lift. She was rewarded by Tyler's deep laughter. Her stomach tingled.

"Starbucks or Seattle's Best?"

"Folgers," she replied simply.

"Folgers?" Tyler looked at her as if she'd just said she liked to drink liquid gold.

"Yes, Folgers. I prefer the simple things in life." But rarely get to enjoy them, she thought. Every morning after Steven left for work she dumped out the pot of expensive Italian-roast coffee, rinsed her unfinished cup, and brewed a pot of plain old black coffee. She drank it while reading the paper or simply watching *Good Morning America*. Watching Robin Roberts was more like it.

"I don't mean to be rude, but you live in Lakeshore, fly around in a private plane, and own your own island, for God's sake. That doesn't sound simple to me."

When she didn't answer, Tyler said quickly, "Oh, shit, that was a stupid, insensitive, rude thing to say. It's really none of my business."

"No, that's okay. You have a very good point. I do all of that, yes, but those are Steven's things, not mine." For some reason Kristin felt the need to explain herself to Tyler. "I would much prefer a four-bedroom house with a big wrap-around front porch on an acre or two. I'd have a John Deer lawn tractor, an old truck for hauling stuff, a Jeep for fun, and season tickets to the Mets, not the Met." Kristin stopped and took a breath. Where in the hell had that come from, and how did she let it come out of her mouth?

Out of the corner of her eye, she saw Tyler staring at her. Her stomach jumped again. What was the matter with her? Between last night and just now, she had practically told her life's fantasy to an almost-total stranger. What was next? Confessing she kissed Pam Counsel in the ninth grade? Now that would be something to talk about.

"What?" Kristin finally said, looking at Tyler. She saw Tyler slowly recover from her shock.

"I guess I never imagined you that way."

"How did you imagine me?" Kristin asked impulsively. Tyler's eyes widened, then turned very dark. Kristin was close enough to see the flicks of blue around the pupil. She could get lost in those eyes. She couldn't remember who said that the eyes were the windows to the soul. And right now what she saw in Tyler's eyes reflected how she felt. It took her breath away.

"How'd it turn out? The stranded-on-a-desert-island dream?"

Kristin wasn't expecting the shift in topic so it took her a second or two to get her mind out of Tyler's arms and back to the here and now.

"I always woke up."

Kristin didn't know if several seconds or several minutes passed before either of them spoke again. Her eyes were locked on Tyler's, occasionally drifting to her lips. Tyler inhaled sharply when she inadvertently licked her own. She started to sway toward Tyler.

"Kristin!" Steven called from behind her, jolting her back to reality. What in the hell was just about to happen? She didn't want to think about it. Couldn't think about it. Steven called for her again. With a sigh, she started to get up.

"Duty calls," she said, and walked away feeling like that was exactly what it was.

CHAPTER THIRTEEN

I'll go."
   "No, you won't. You need to stay here."
Kristin visibly flinched when her husband spoke.
What a bully, Tyler thought.

It was a few hours before noon and Tyler wanted to explore as much as possible before the heat of the day set in. If they didn't find some type of shelter they would have to expand their makeshift lean-to to keep the intense rays of the island sun from beating down on them. That and they had to find fresh water or they'd be in bigger trouble. Kristin had been the only one to speak up when Tyler asked if anyone wanted to double back in the direction she and Paul had gone yesterday.

Of course nobody said anything, which didn't surprise Tyler. This time instead of everyone standing in front of her trying to pretend she hadn't spoken, they were sprawled in various poses around the campsite. They had to have heard her so that wasn't why no one volunteered.

"Thanks, but you shouldn't go by yourself." Tyler waited and looked around, not expecting anyone to volunteer. In fact, she would have bet the house on it.

Kristin was visibly disappointed and looked like she might say more but changed her mind. How many times a day did Kristin do that? Tyler's anger boiled but this wasn't the time or place, or even any of her business.

"I guess that settles it. Paul and I'll be gone a couple of hours. If we're not back by one, send out a search party," she said flippantly, knowing damn good and well no one would volunteer for that either. "We'll see if we can find a better place to camp other than out here in the open on the beach. And we have to find some fresh water," she told Kristin, the only one who seemed to be paying attention.

Kristin stepped closer, and Tyler's stomach jumped as she imagined Kristen kissing her good-bye every morning as she went off to work. Who was she kidding? Her office was in her house, she usually worked in the evenings, and, most important, Kristin was married to Steven. But all that aside, she still tingled inside.

"Be careful," Kristin said quietly. "I don't want anything to happen to you."

"Neither do I," Tyler answered, not quite sure where her inane response came from. Paul was standing beside her and she reached for his arm. "I have Paul with me. We'll be fine. Don't wait up," she said lightly over her shoulder as she and he walked down the beach.

"What is going on with you two?" Paul asked when they were once again out of earshot. "The sparks between you and my boss's wife are visible in the bright light of day."

Tyler thought for a moment about playing dumb, but Paul knew better and she was tired of pretending. It had been a long twenty-four hours, and if they couldn't signal a plane or passing ship, it would only get longer.

"Nothing." It wasn't a lie. Nothing was going on between them. She was safe with that response, at least for now.

"Nothing, my skinny, queer butt," he said, slowing his walk so she could keep up more easily. "I may be blind about a lot of things, but I know girl-on-girl when I see it."

Tyler tried not to stumble. She glanced over her shoulder and saw that, like yesterday, they were out of the others' sight. She didn't try to hide her limp anymore. "God damn, my leg hurts. Let's sit." She motioned to a large rock to their right.

She didn't immediately answer Paul's question and knew he'd press her again. He wasn't the type to let things go, definitely not with her. She busily wiped the dirt and sand from the bottom of her leg. Her quadriceps burned with fatigue, and her stump ached from the constant jarring caused by walking in the sand.

"Nothing's going on between me and Kristin. We talked during our shift on watch and then again this morning. Nothing more. Just being friendly and helpful, and trying to get through this." Again not a lie.

"But you wanted to do more."

"No, I didn't." Okay, that was a lie.

"Tyler, I saw you two on the beach. It looked like one more second and she was going to kiss you."

Tyler jerked her head up so fast she got dizzy. "What are you talking about? She was going to do no such thing."

Paul laughed at her. "And you say I'm blind. She was *definitely* going to kiss you. Mmm huh, yes sirree, ma'am. She was going to plant one on you."

"Shut up, Paul. You don't know what you're talking about. Kristin's married to that asshole boss of yours, for what reason completely evades me, and most important is not interested in me." But if she were…Tyler's blood raced and she mentally cursed herself for such ridiculous thoughts.

"Who cares? Half the lesbians I know were married once, some of them two or three times, trying to find the magic."

Tyler stood, not wanting to continue this conversation. "For God's sake, Paul, she is not interested in me so just drop it. We've got more important things to do other than speculate on Kristin Walker's sexual proclivities. Like survive."

Paul laughed at her again. "Sexual proclivities? Tyler, my dear, have you ever heard the phrase, 'She doth protest too much'?"

"The correct phrase, 'The lady doth protest too much, methinks,' does not apply in this case." The famous phrase from *Hamlet* had been interpreted to mean that it would be a lot more believable if the lady weren't so vocal about her innocence. Or, the more you try to talk your way out of it, the less people believe you. Surely she wasn't that.

Paul simply laughed at her again. "You just keep telling yourself that, my friend. Just keep telling yourself that."

Tyler focused on putting one foot in front of the other in the soft sand. The sun was beating on the back of her neck and she knew the tops of her ears would burn. She was hungry, thirsty, and filthy, but she couldn't get her mind off Kristin. She wanted to spend more time with her, but based on the conversation last night and this morning, as well as her growing attraction to Kristin, she knew she shouldn't. Tyler didn't want to even think about her body's visceral reaction to Kristin.

Was Paul right? Had Kristin been about to kiss her? Jesus, when? She replayed their conversation last night and this morning. Sure, Kristin had revealed probably more than she intended, but that in no way was a prelude to a kiss. *People don't normally talk about their sad life and then kiss someone, do they?* How in the hell would she know? She'd dated Jessica for years, and since the accident she hadn't been with another woman except for the time it took to get her clothes off. Was she that far out of touch?

They'd been walking only about fifteen minutes when Tyler heard the sound of running water. Paul must have heard it at the same time because he looked at her with a huge grin and they both dashed to their left.

It was a scene from a movie. The waterfall had to be at least thirty feet high, falling into a large pool, ripples spreading out to the edges. Trees and vines surrounded the area, a canopy overhead shadowing half of the pond from the sun's harsh rays. Flat rocks around the perimeter looked as though someone had set them by hand in a perfect semicircle.

"Do you think it's fresh?" Paul asked, stepping closer.

"Probably, but there's only one way to find out." Tyler knelt down and scooped up a handful. The water was cool and crystal clear. It looked inviting and she tentatively took a sip. She licked her lips a few times.

"It's not seawater," she said, grateful she hadn't just swallowed a mouthful of salty or brackish water. She took another mouthful, the cool liquid as refreshing as it looked. "Don't drink too much," she warned Paul. "It might not be fresh, and you might get a terrible case of diarrhea or puke everywhere."

"Do you have to be so graphic?" Paul wiped his hand on his pants after sipping some.

"If I'd said gastrointestinal-tract disturbance, would it make a difference? The result would still be the same. And I don't want to be anywhere near you when it does," she added jokingly. She untied her shoes and slipped them off, along with her socks.

"What are you doing?" Paul asked.

Tyler pulled her shirt over her head. "Getting in. I stink, I'm sticky, and I've got to clean Lucy. I'm going to take advantage and take a nature bath. Get over here and help me." She dropped her pants and underwear in one move. Tyler wasn't shy about being naked around Paul. He'd seen her in the buff several times, and right now she didn't care who saw her.

She removed her prosthesis and, with Paul's help, hopped on one foot into the cool water. It felt fabulous. She sighed as it slid over her hot body. She floated to the center of the pond and ducked her head. She ran her fingers through her short hair, making a mental note to next time bring the shampoo that was neatly packed in her backpack. Luckily Paul had managed to get most of their luggage out of the plane.

Paul's girly laugh gave him away just before he splashed her from behind. "Oh, man, this feels great." He swam around in front of her. "Do we have to tell anybody about this?"

"Only if we can stand their smell, which I, for one, don't even want to think about. Besides, if it is okay to drink we'll need it."

"You're right. A boy can dream, can't he?" Paul asked before dipping below the water level.

They swam for a few more minutes before Tyler said, "I'm getting out. We can dry off on one of those rocks over there in the sun." She pointed at several rocks large enough to lie on comfortably. "Then we have to go tell everybody."

"Do we have to?" Paul whined, not really serious.

Tyler was able to get out of the water and onto the rock without Paul's assistance. She lay down, the rock warming her back, the sun on her face. She had taken Lucy into the water with her to rinse the sand and grit from the inside, and she placed it on the rock beside her to dry. She heard Paul get out and they lay not speaking, the water evaporating off their skin.

❖

At first she thought a pesky fly was buzzing around her face. Tyler waved it away and it returned, this time more forcefully. She was about to swat at it again when soft lips covered hers. Her heart jumped at the same time her eyes flew open. The woman kissing her, and, yes, she instantly knew it was a woman, was too close for Tyler to see clearly. That and the fact that she was a bit farsighted. But the owner of the soft lips, whoever she was, certainly knew how to use them.

Tyler didn't have a chance to kiss back, the woman's lips and tongue fluttering around her, nipping, sucking, and biting just enough for her to want more. Tyler's hands instinctively moved from the warm rock into the woman's hair. It was thick yet silky and felt like fine grains of sand as it slid through her fingers.

Tyler pressed the stranger's mouth to hers firmly, leaving no doubt that she wanted to continue the kisses. After a few moments, Tyler changed her mind and gently pulled away. She wanted to see who was kissing her, needed to know whose mouth was one kiss away from making her lose all reason, all sense of sanity. She hadn't been kissed like this in a long, long time.

When the woman lifted her head Tyler's heart jumped into her throat. The woman gazed directly at her, eyes dark, desire burning her pupils wide. She didn't waver or look away like most women. It always surprised Tyler how many women could make love to you yet not look you in the eye. But not this woman. Not Kristin Walker. The bold want clearly visible in her eyes absolutely took Tyler's breath away.

Kristin said nothing. She didn't have to. Tyler was so far gone in the depths of her eyes, the promise of pleasure they conveyed, that words were unnecessary. Tyler couldn't have spoken even if she wanted to.

Tyler held Kristin's head in her hands but didn't pull her lips back to hers. She wanted to, desperately. Wanted to ravish the mouth that hovered not more than an inch from hers, explore it to the fullest, then do it again and again and again. Tyler suddenly realized she had wanted to kiss Kristin for years, and now that she was right where she wanted her, she did nothing.

Kristin held her gaze and Tyler's breathing became shallow and fast. It was as if Kristin was making love to her with only her eyes. The burning started somewhere deep inside her, streaking out to her limbs, fingertips, then back again. Tyler was on fire and Kristin hadn't even touched her.

She hadn't been in this position since her accident. She was always the one in charge in sexual situations, the aggressor, the one leaning over, the top, to use a tired label. She called the shots, decided who got naked, who came first, who kissed who where. She had always felt totally defenseless on her back and now, after the accident, that was definitely the case. But she felt none of that now. Kristin was in control and Tyler was not afraid.

With deliberate patience Kristin lowered her head. She stopped when only a breath separated them, and Tyler thought she would die if Kristin didn't kiss her again. That she would shrivel up and blow away in the ocean breeze if those lips didn't cover hers again. She opened her mouth. She'd beg if she had to, but didn't have the chance before Kristin was kissing her again.

This time, her kisses were different. Still exploring, yes, yet demanding Tyler participate in return. Tyler, always one not to be left behind, took up the gauntlet Kristin held in front of her and wrapped her fingers in her hair. Their tongues met in a wild dance of desire, fighting for control then releasing it to receive pleasure. Back and forth they dueled, until they were breathless.

Kristin lifted her head and used her wonderful mouth to trail kisses across Tyler's cheek and face. This was about the time where Tyler would flip their positions and lead her and her partner down the slippery slope to mutual fulfillment, but she didn't have the strength or the need this time. Instead she arched her neck, giving Kristin free access to whatever she wanted. And Kristin took it.

Kristin trailed damp kisses in a path up and down her neck. Kristin found the hot spot just below her left earlobe and tormented her with her tongue for what felt like an eternity. Kristin seemed to know when she needed a kiss and always returned to her lips for another searing expression of desire.

Each trip down her neck, Kristin ventured a little farther. Kristin didn't hesitate a single beat as first her hands, then her mouth explored Tyler's body. Nimble fingers ran up and down her side, passing lightly over her stomach and between her breasts. Her nipples ached to be touched and Kristin's hand passed closer each time.

Tyler was in agony. She wanted to be touched, needed to feel Kristin's lips on her nipple, sucking and biting until she begged for mercy. But she did nothing. Any other time she would have made it very clear that was what she needed, and on more than one occasion she took matters into her own hands and put the woman's mouth or hand exactly where she needed it. But not with Kristin.

The teasing and anticipation was driving Tyler crazy. She no longer could remain still and let Kristin do all the work, have all the fun. Her hands began their own exploration, running up and down Kristin's firm back. Tyler had no idea where Kristin's clothes were and didn't care. She did care about how soft and warm her skin was.

Kristin gasped as her nipple lightly grazed Tyler's stomach. An instant later Kristin was kissing her again, their breasts pressed together. Kristin slid her leg between hers and Tyler felt the wetness of her desire. God, it had been so long since she felt the wonderful warmth of another woman like this. This was not the most intimate of positions, but the unmistakable evidence of desire was breathtaking. With Kristin it was unspeakable beauty.

Kristin shifted slightly and finally her hand cupped Tyler's breast. Her own nipple hardened even more than she thought possible when Kristin's thumb brushed over it. Tyler's body unconsciously followed the touch wanting much, much more. Finally Kristin lifted her head and left a trail of kisses surrounding the perimeter of her breast, each circle moving closer to her nipple.

Kristin's hot breath tickled the hard peak and Tyler was afraid she would come. She didn't want to, it was too soon, but she needed the release. As if sensing her indecision, Kristin covered her nipple with her mouth. Tyler moaned in pleasure, the first sound coming from either of them since their first kiss.

Kristin sucked and bit and licked the erect point, and Tyler wrapped her fingers into Kristin's hair even tighter. The familiar burn started low in her belly and exploded before Tyler knew what was happening. Never before had she come like this, certainly not this fast. Before she had a chance to think, Kristin transferred her attention to her other breast with the same effect.

Tyler was stunned by her body's reaction. She was typically a one-orgasm girl, and to have two without even being touched astounded her. What was happening to her? Who was this woman making love to her, and what had she done with the Tyler she knew?

Kristin slid down her belly, peppering her stomach with more hot kisses. Tyler tensed when she reached the scar on her stomach, but Kristin didn't stop and ask about it or even hesitate in her journey south. It didn't take any persuasion for Kristin to spread her legs. Tyler was more than ready but didn't know if she could come again. Two was unusual, three would be a damn miracle.

Kristin wasn't timid with her touch. Confidently she let her hands and fingers explore Tyler with as much attention as she had everything else. In five years Tyler had never let a woman get this far. Hell, she never let a woman take her clothes off below the waist. She only let hands and fingers inside her pants, and never, never had their hands wandered any farther. When Kristin's tongue flicked her clitoris, Tyler said something but had no idea what. She didn't think it was crude or stupid because Kristin chuckled and smiled against her. When Kristin's mouth settled on her, Tyler pulled her closer.

Kristin's tongue moved up and down over the stiff shaft, and Tyler thought her head would explode. Her fingers clenched, her toes curled, every nerve ending was alive. Her breath caught in her throat. She was on the verge of her third orgasm and had never felt this alive. Kristin drew back slightly, and when she put first one, then a second finger into her, Tyler detonated.

Tyler's ass lifted off the rock with each convulsion. Waves of orgasm pulsed through her with every beat of her heart. Bright lights exploded behind her eyes, the roar in her ears deafening. She couldn't breathe, couldn't think, could only feel. She rode every surge and swell until her body could give no more.

A sharp pain in her back made her open her eyes. She expected to see Kristin, but what she saw shocked her even more. No one. Absolutely no one. Sitting up she grabbed her clothes and looked around.

Paul was lightly snoring. Tyler rubbed her hand across her face. Holy Christ, she'd been dreaming.

CHAPTER FOURTEEN

Thank God," Kristin said, hands clasped in front of her. Tyler and Paul had been gone longer than they had yesterday, and she had been pacing back and forth waiting for them to return. The news that they had found fresh water almost made up for her worry.

"Where is it? Is it fresh? Can we drink it? Can we bathe in it? Are there fish in it?" The questions pummeled Tyler and Paul.

"About twenty minutes from here, yes, yes, if we're careful, yes, downstream, and I didn't see any," Tyler replied, her voice a little shaky.

Tyler wouldn't look at her, not even a glance. Her eyes darted back and forth at everyone else but never at her. This wasn't like her. Tyler always looked directly at her, not at all shy or hesitant. And earlier this morning when they talked at the water's edge, Kristin felt like Tyler could see right into her soul. Now she wouldn't even look at her. What was going on? Had something happened? Had she upset Tyler?

"We found a lot of wood for the fire and a couple of places that are much better than this," Tyler indicated their meager campsite, "for shelter. Everybody grab as much as you can carry, and once we get set up you can bathe and change clothes. That'll make you feel better, and we can think a little more clearly and make a few more decisions."

"Will we still be close enough to the beach to keep the fire going?" Kristin asked. Tyler had stressed the importance of keeping their signal fire burning, and she wasn't about to let it go out. Not if it was their best chance to be rescued.

Finally Tyler looked at her, then just as quickly turned away. "Yes, we will be. The trees will give us good cover, especially from this sun." Tyler lifted her hand and covered her eyes as she looked into the cloudless sky. "It's the best we've seen so far. Maybe we'll find something better in the next few days, but for now it'll do."

Tyler's aloofness puzzled Kristin. Had she said something last night or this morning to upset her? What could have happened from the time she and Paul left that caused such a change? Suddenly Kristin felt cold and empty.

Tyler made her feel safe, alive, and important. She listened to what she had to say, surprised that Tyler said anything to her at all. Kristin didn't have many friends and none that she would have confided in the way she had with Tyler in the last twenty-four hours. What about Tyler compelled her to open up and share her thoughts? Thoughts she barely let herself think about, let alone tell anyone. The stress leading up to this trip and the crash obviously were causing her to slip.

"You heard the lady, fresh water, let's get going," Robert said. Kristin hid her shock as he gathered up a few blankets and two of the suitcases. The others quickly followed his lead, arms full of the gear they had managed to get out of the plane.

"I'll get them headed in the right direction, then we'll come back and get you, Steven," Paul said, glancing at Kristin before looking at his boss.

They all followed Paul for several hundred yards, and Kristin thought they looked like little ducklings following mama duck. Tyler had stayed behind.

"Somebody help me, goddamn it," Steven growled. He was sitting up, his face white with pain. Kristin knew he hadn't slept much last night, tossing and turning as his limited ability allowed. He hadn't kept her awake, but she hadn't slept much.

She had been fully attuned to Tyler, fifteen feet from her. She and Paul lay on the opposite side of the fire, giving Kristin just enough light to see their silhouette. They weren't sleeping as close to each other as the other couples, who huddled together as if protecting each other from the unknown. Steven didn't want anyone near him, fearing someone would bump his broken leg. Even without his injury and due to an extra-large king-size bed they hadn't slept within touching distance in a long, long time.

Tyler approached, her limp not as noticeable as before. She was pleased that Tyler wasn't in pain, at least not as much. For the third or fourth time Kristin wondered what caused it. Maybe Tyler would tell her. She doubted it. Not the way she'd been acting toward her since this morning. Tyler continued to intentionally evade her and walked directly toward Steven.

"Seems as though your loyal and devoted staff are more interested in a bath than you. Come on, I'll help you." Tyler knelt, putting one of Steven's arms around her shoulders.

Kristin couldn't just do nothing. Here was this extraordinary woman, with no ties to Steven, helping him move. She mimicked Tyler's actions and they had him standing in just a few moments.

"Thanks," Kristin said gratefully.

They started in the direction of the others and Steven cussed and complained with every step. Kristin was tired of hearing him. Obviously Steven was in pain, but she couldn't muster up the energy or the interest to feel sympathetic.

After only a dozen yards Kristin was exhausted from not enough sleep and practically carrying Steven through the thick sand. Who was she kidding? Tyler had borne most of Steven's immense weight; she had just helped support him.

Paul was on his way back to them and started jogging when he saw them. He was out of breath when he reached them. "Jesus, Tyler. Why didn't you wait for me?"

Kristin read his expression of concern as he took Tyler's place next to Steven. She felt a pang of something she might call jealousy.

"I'm all right," Tyler said, even though Kristin could see the pain reflected around the corners of her mouth.

"Yeah, right, and I'm Dorothy from *The Wizard of Oz*. Sometimes you're so stubborn," Paul scolded her.

"Don't go there, Paul," Tyler warned him.

"Too late, sweetie, I'm already there."

"Then turn around or back up because you won't like the view," Tyler replied.

Kristin watched and listened as they traded words. Both were serious, yet respectful. Whereas her arguments with Steven were often one-sided, his words ripping through her, Paul and Kristin's were more like verbal sparring. Back and forth they went, each feeding off the other until Kristin wasn't sure who'd won. But their interchange didn't seem to have anything to do with winning or losing. It appeared to be simple, healthy disagreement.

"Can we make a stretcher or something to carry him on instead?" Kristin asked. "Would that be easier?"

"Probably not," Tyler responded. She and Paul had stumbled through the sand, often forced to stop and rest. Kristin had tried to spell Tyler several times, but Tyler politely refused, insisting she was fine.

Kristin heard the water before she saw it. The roar of the waterfall grew louder as they neared. Steven was practically unconscious now and absolutely dead weight, and they barely managed to get him to the new camp.

The new camp was at the base of a small peninsula, jutting out several hundred yards from the main beach. It was the perfect place, at least as best as Kristin could tell. It was close enough to the water to watch for a passing ship, yet provided them with enough cover from the elements. The trees were thick, the constant wind from the sea shaping them into an almost-perfect canopy. If their situation wasn't so dire, this place could be the ideal setting for a romantic getaway.

The others had dropped their supplies haphazardly into scattered piles. Obviously no one had paid any attention to how or why she had organized things the way she had the day before.

"Can't depend on them to do anything," Paul muttered, looking around the site. "I left them with specific instructions to set up just like we had it. Guess they were more interested in taking a bath than making sure we were prepared."

"What a surprise," Tyler said sarcastically.

Steven moaned as they laid him in the shade and didn't stir after they tucked a blanket around him. Kristin thanked them for what felt like the hundredth time. Other than Kristin, Paul, and, of course, Tyler, no one had lifted a finger to help. So much for company loyalty, she thought. But weren't they a lot like him? What kind of loyalty did Steven instill in the people around him? The last twenty-four hours had proved that he ruled more through fear and intimidation than respect. Why had it taken this experience for her to see it so clearly?

Kristin helped Tyler and Paul organize the supplies, and before too long the three of them had their new home in order. Kristin often helped Tyler, her limp more pronounced than ever, her movements slowing. What little food they had was off the ground, the bottles of water, soda, and juice nestled in a cool place in the nook of a tree. The luggage was grouped according to couple, the remaining miscellaneous items they had scavenged from the plane in another area.

One by one everyone returned to the camp. Kristin was irritated that no one mentioned the work they had done to get the camp in order. But why should they? If they hadn't stayed to help why would it even occur to them? They were so used to people doing everything for them they didn't even see it anymore. How sad was that?

Had she become one of those people? She didn't think so. She always thanked the yard guys, offering them a glass of lemonade when the weather was hot. If Steven knew he would probably fire them and throw out all the glasses they might have used. For the last four or five years she'd added a little something to the monthly payment during the holidays.

Since her dream earlier this morning, Tyler was more than aware of Kristin's proximity. The dream had rattled her and made her hypersensitive to Kristin. Who was she kidding? She'd been aware of everything about Kristin since the first time they met. Her smile, when she *really* smiled, was breathtaking. Her hands were strong, with fingers long and perfectly shaped. Her dream told her just how perfect those fingers could be, and she couldn't suppress the shudder that ran through her.

"Are you all right?" Kristin asked, touching her arm.

Shock waves pierced her exhaustion and the pain in her leg, making her jump. Kristin jerked her hand back as if Tyler had burned her.

"I'm sorry," Kristin said immediately. "I shouldn't have done that."

The shock and fear on Kristin's face tore at Tyler's stomach, and she grabbed her hand before it was out of reach. The reconnection was as powerful as their first contact.

"No, it's all right. It just startled me, that's all."

Tyler couldn't take her eyes away from Kristin's. She felt herself being pulled into the depths and didn't even try to fight it. Images of her dream flashed back and Tyler wanted to drown inside her. Tyler caressed the top of Kristin's hand with her thumb. She envisioned the rise and fall of her knuckles as the curve of her hip, the backs of her knees, and the swell of her breast. Tyler's breathing shifted from fast to shallow as the burn in her stomach shifted to deep in her groin.

She watched Kristin's expression transform from fear to confusion, then to shock, and finally to something Tyler couldn't recognize. This time Kristin quickly drew her hand away.

"I'd better check on Steven." Kristin didn't meet her eyes. She turned away and covered the ground between them and where Steven still lay unconscious.

"Holy shit, you are in t-r-o-u-b-l-e," Paul said. "Big trouble." He was standing beside her, shaking his head with an occasional "tsk, tsk" thrown in to accentuate his point.

"Shut up," Tyler managed to say. Emotions raced through her body, each vying for the number-one spot for her attention. Tyler had never experienced such a battle and didn't know what to do. This didn't even resemble her reaction to Jessica or any of the other women she had met. Even those she had taken to bed had not affected her like this physically. They were a mere flicker compared to the desire that burned through her for Kristin. Paul was right. She was in big trouble.

CHAPTER FIFTEEN

The water was cool and Kristin stepped in cautiously. She had learned to swim as a child but was never completely comfortable in the water. Their pool at home was only five feet deep, and even though she was six inches taller than that, she could never completely relax in it.

This pond frightened her. She could see her feet but was hesitant nonetheless. But she was dirty and had sand in places she'd rather not think about. She was determined to overcome her fear, especially after her humiliating experience getting out of the plane. Slowly she waded out until the water rose just above her knees. That was far enough, she thought, splashing the refreshing stuff on her arms. She had changed into a pair of shorts and tank top, skinny-dipping definitely out of the question.

She sat on a large boulder, the water reaching just above her waist. Gathering her growing courage she leaned her head back, dipping her hair in the water, running her fingers through it. Out of the corner of her eye she saw her blond tresses billow around her. After a few more swishes she lifted her head, water dripping down her back.

She cupped the chilly water in her palms and spread it over her face. Maybe this will cool me off, she thought. Her skin still felt hot. Obviously I need it. What in the hell is wrong with me? What happened back in the camp with Tyler? She looked pale and was visibly shaken. Kristin had simply expressed her concern.

Kristin hadn't anticipated the effect of her touch. She hadn't really thought at all, but Tyler's reaction immediately told her she shouldn't have done it.

Tyler reacted as if something very hot had touched her. Kristin jerked away, but the look on Tyler's face completely confused her. She was even more surprised when Tyler reclaimed her hand, and this time when she looked at Tyler, Kristin knew exactly what was going on. Any woman with any experience whatsoever could read Tyler's desire. But her own reaction had turned Kristin's world upside down.

Over the years, she had been on the receiving side of desire from other women and, other than feeling slightly flattered, had otherwise not been interested. Not in the slightest. But that was definitely not the case with Tyler Logan.

Kristin studied her hand, the one Tyler had held. She ran her thumb over the knuckles just as Tyler had, and it was her turn to shudder. She swallowed hard, suddenly feeling light-headed and dizzy.

This couldn't be happening. She was married to Steven, and Tyler and Paul were together. Or were they? Kristin reflected on her observations of them, as well as their unusual relationship. True, it wasn't what she'd been used to, but every couple had their own connection.

She shook her head quickly, water spraying out in every direction. "No," she said out loud, trying to convince herself. No way could she be interested in a woman, let alone this one. There were Steven, Paul, and the undeniable fact that Tyler was a woman. Talk about three strikes and you're out. She would never take a man away from a woman, would never do that to another woman. But that made no sense either. She didn't want Paul, she wanted Tyler.

Now that she had finally admitted it to herself, everything fell into place. Why she looked forward to her social responsibilities when she knew Tyler would be present. The way she always knew exactly where Tyler was when they were at the same function. The way she just felt happier and more like a woman whenever Tyler looked at her.

If Steven had any idea he would kill her. Well, maybe that was a little strong, but she shuddered at the thought of the scene he would make. In the last few years she'd had a nagging thought in the back of her mind that one day Steven would hit her. Actually she was surprised that he hadn't already. Would that be the nudge that pushed her over the edge to leave him? Was she waiting for it and, if so, how pathetic was that? If she was not in love with Steven anymore, if she ever really had been, then what was she waiting for? Why did she stay? She could support herself. It would be tough in the beginning, but with a lot of hard work and a little luck she'd be fine. Was she afraid of scandal? What would she tell her parents, their friends? What friends? They didn't have any friends; they were all Steven's.

Question after question raced through her brain, each more complicated than the last. The sheer enormity of what she had just recognized overwhelmed her. She didn't know where to start, what to do. And she was stuck on this island for who knew how long with Steven, Paul, and Tyler. They needed to depend on each other to get through this ordeal. They were battling life and death, and here she was lusting over one of them. A woman at that.

"Wait a minute," Kristin said to herself, an idea forming. "It's just infatuation, that's it. Between reading every Blake Hudson book several times and Tyler taking command of our situation, so to speak, I've transferred my hero worship from Blake to Tyler." The fact that Tyler was almost a carbon copy of Blake added to her explanation. Or was it the other way around? Did the author shape the character or the character shape the author?

Kristin worked really hard to convince herself but gave up when she realized she was just making excuses. It was true. She wanted Tyler. To feel her touch again, hear her laugh, experience her kisses. "Oh, no," she said, dropping her face into her hands. What in the hell am I going to do now?

❖

Tyler hadn't meant to spy. She just wanted to make sure Kristin didn't run into any trouble along the way. At least that's what she told herself as she followed Kristin to the water. What a liar, she thought. A big, fat liar.

The foliage around the pool at the base of the waterfall was thick, giving Tyler ample places to observe without being discovered. Kristin seemed to be hesitant about going into the pool but then took a deep breath and slowly waded in. She didn't go all the way in, like Tyler and Paul had, but stayed near the outer edge. It looked like she was afraid.

"I've gotcha," Tyler whispered silently, as if Kristin could hear her and relax. She wouldn't let anything happen to Kristin. She'd make sure Kristin could bathe in safety and comfort. And what would she do if she had to do something? Jump out of her hiding place and save the day? Then Kristin would know she'd been spying. Talk about getting your hand caught in the cookie jar.

Tyler was half hoping she would strip but knew Kristin wouldn't be comfortable doing so. Her mouth watered as she watched the water slide over Kristin's arms. She imagined her hands running over Kristin's body, her mouth stopping the water that trickled between Kristin's breasts. She practically stopped breathing when Kristin dipped her head in the water.

Her back was arched, her neck exposed, and Tyler wanted to run her lips and tongue over the exposed flesh. She wanted to touch Kristin, make her bend like that in pure pleasure. Her palms itched to caress the two perfectly shaped mounds on Kristin's chest. She forced herself not to walk out of her hiding place and make her fantasy a reality.

But Kristin was married, and she was married to Paul's boss. No one would come out unscathed in this little soap opera. And how could she forget the fact that, other than Jessica, no one had ever seen her with one leg? And we all know how that turned out, she mused ruefully. The thought of her leg repulsing Kristin sobered her. What a cluster fuck. How had she gotten here?

Tyler thought Kristin was crying when she put her face in her hands. Who wouldn't, at this point? The last day had been one out of the pages of a fiction novel or a movie starring Tom Hanks, not what Kristin was used to. They weren't dreaming on custom-set sleep-number beds, or sitting under a big umbrella sipping fruity drinks, on the side table a Waterford plate filled with caviar in the middle, crackers perfectly lining the edge.

No, they were bathing in freezing water, eating peanuts and granola bars, and sleeping on the ground. Tyler's anger at Steven returned. She was not meant to be in this situation, but because of his arrogance, stupidity, and all the other things Tyler could name to blame Steven, it was still his fault.

Kristin stood and turned Tyler's way. Her damp clothes left nothing to the imagination, and Tyler lost her footing. She grabbed a branch to keep from falling, the leaves rustling. She held her breath, praying Kristin didn't notice, but God didn't hear her prayer this time.

"Who is it? Who's there?" Kristin called in alarm.

"Kristin?" Tyler said, pretending to be approaching the water instead of acknowledging the fact that she was a peeping Tom. "Kristin, it's Tyler. Are you here?" Her ruse worked because she saw Kristin visibly relax.

"Yes, over here by the water," Kristin replied, hurrying to her towel and wrapping it around her, hiding the tantalizing view.

"There you are," Tyler said, pretending it was the first time she'd seen her instead of watching like a voyeur for fifteen minutes. "You shouldn't just wander off. You need to tell somebody where you're going."

"I'm sorry," Kristin responded, wringing the water from her hair. "I guess I was just so intent on getting clean I wasn't thinking. It won't happen again."

Kristin wouldn't look at her, like a kid being punished. "I wasn't fussing, just being cautious," Tyler said, trying to erase the look of shame. "What if you'd sprained your ankle or fallen into a ravine or something?" Tyler suppressed a shudder at the thought.

"You're right. It was a stupid thing to do."

Tyler didn't think, just acted. She stepped in front of Kristin and put her finger under her chin, lifting her head. Kristin still wouldn't meet her eyes. "You're not stupid, Kristin. I just don't want you to get hurt." Couldn't stand it if you got seriously hurt or even died, she wanted to add, but caught herself just in time.

"I understand and I appreciate your concern. Like I said, it won't happen again."

Tyler didn't stop Kristin as she walked away. Her pace was quick, as if she couldn't wait to get away from Tyler, which was probably for the best. Tyler needed to stop acting impulsively when it came to Kristin. Nothing good would come of it. On the contrary, it could only lead to disaster.

CHAPTER SIXTEEN

I'm not going to be responsible if anything happens to you."
Steven sneered at Tyler.

Her patience with him expired. Her leg throbbed, she was hot, tired, and so keyed up over Kristin she lashed out. "It's been over twenty years since I've had anyone responsible for me, Steven, and I'm sure as shit not starting with you."

His eyes were hot with anger. "You can't talk to me like that."

"Yes, I can, and if you don't shut the fuck up and give everyone, including your wife, some respect, I'll leave you, you sorry excuse for a man, to rot here on this beach." Her comment was uncalled for but she didn't care.

She had mentioned she was going to see if she could catch something to eat when Steven made his ridiculous comment.

"Just how long do you think we can survive on bags of peanuts and Diet Coke, Steven? Do you think a helicopter is headed our way with a parachute filled with lobster tails? No one even knows we're missing."

"What?" Robert asked. All of them were watching the ugly exchange.

"Nothing," Steven barked. He was good at that. It seemed to be his preferred communication style.

Tyler refused to let him off the hook. "I said no one has any clue we're missing. No one on the island is expecting us, so no one will report us missing for another four days. Isn't that right, Steven?"

Steven glared at Kristin, and Tyler immediately regretted her outburst. Usually she thought before she spoke, but she was becoming more unlike herself lately. "Did you get a Mayday out?" she asked, trying to deflect Steven's attention from the fact that Kristin was the only one who could have supplied Tyler with that piece of information.

"Well, did you?" She repeated the question. "I didn't think so," she said quickly, picking up on Steven's expression. "So, unless you have a better idea of how we're going to survive for at least four more days, I'm going fishing. I'm hungry and it's only going to get worse." She stepped closer to Steven, standing directly over him. "And I get very cranky when I'm hungry."

"I'll go with you," Paul volunteered.

Tyler turned and looked from one person to the other with an expression on her face that she knew conveyed the question, "Anybody else?" Shaking her head in disgust she grabbed the stick she'd whittled to a point and walked away.

❖

If Tyler could have been an observer, she suspected she would have watched a scene unfold in front of her similar to the one in the movie *Castaway*. She was up to her knees in the water, moving as slowly as she could so as not to startle the school of fish swimming in the low tide. She held the makeshift spear in her right hand, high above her head, ready to strike. And just like in the movie, she missed more often than she hit.

Even with Paul's help it took several hours to spear three fish. She fell more times than she could remember, cutting her leg on the jagged rocks. Her face was sunburned, the blood from her knee still dripped down her shin, and her shoes were full of sand. She tried not to think about the effect of the salt water on her prosthesis. It wasn't as if she had any choice about getting it wet. If she left it to the others, they'd all starve because of their pride, indignation, or whatever was so far up their butt it prevented them from helping.

Tyler knew Kristin would volunteer, but Steven had silenced her with a scathing look before she had the chance.

She didn't want Kristin around, didn't want to fight the desire to take her in her arms and kiss the hell out of her. She wanted to roll around in the waves, laughing and making love like a very different scene in a very different movie. But she didn't have the energy or the desire to fight the temptation so she eliminated the possibility instead.

"You have got to take care of yourself," Paul said, his arm wrapped around Tyler's waist, supporting her.

"I'm fine." That was becoming her standard reply.

"Tyler, it's me. You don't have to put on that tough-girl act. I know you better than that, and you know I won't think less of you if you give in or just slow down a bit."

Paul was right, but as much as she wanted to collapse and let him take care of her like he had years ago, she couldn't. Something inside was driving her, and when she got like that she couldn't do much to stop it.

❖

Tyler was rooting around looking for the first-aid kit. She knew they had one, remembered finding it in the first load Paul and Mark recovered from the plane before it sank. It had to be here. When they moved camps she had double-checked to make sure they weren't leaving anything behind.

"What are you looking for?"

Tyler jumped, not because it was Kristin but because she had been so focused on finding the kit she hadn't heard anyone approach. Although, in her defense, it was hard to hear anyone walking in the sand.

"The first-aid kit," Tyler answered honestly. Her leg was badly cut, and it was extremely important to find an antiseptic. She couldn't risk infection in her only good leg. That could turn into complete disaster. She wasn't worried about Kristin knowing she was injured. But how could anyone not know, the blood leaving a trail of droplets behind her when she walked.

"Here it is," Kristin said, lifting the medium-size white box with the big red cross on the top. "What happened?"

"I fell and cut my leg a little. Nothing serious." Tyler lied.

"I'll be the judge of that. Sit down."

"I can take care of it," Tyler said a little too quickly.

Kristin only pointed to one of the boxes off to the side of the supplies. Tyler acquiesced, more concerned with her leg than arguing.

The sharp rock had torn a hole in her pants, the surrounding material bloody. Kristin didn't hesitate as she ripped the thin fabric to expose the gash on the outside of her right calf.

"Ouch," she said, inspecting it from several angles. "That looks like it really hurts."

"Only when I think about it." Tyler leaned back, her hands resting on a box slightly behind her.

"What about when you don't think about it?" Kristin unlatched the box.

"Then it really, really hurts."

Kristin chuckled. "Yeah, well, this won't make it feel any better," she said, soaking a piece of white gauze with a clear liquid. "Are you going to be brave or do you need something to bite on?"

"That only happens in the movies. However, with you as my nurse I won't feel a thing." And at that moment, the pain immediately disappeared. Kristin was kneeling, looking up at her. Her hair reflected the waning rays of the late-afternoon sun, casting highlights throughout the already light color. Her face was fresh and flawless. Her eyes twinkled with amusement and concern. Her lips were parted in a stunning smile, and Tyler didn't know how to breathe.

She was far too aware of Kristin's proximity to her crotch. Tyler swallowed, remembering the image in her dream of Kristin in this exact same position, her head between her legs. She broke out in a sweat and her hands trembled.

Kristin furrowed her brow. "Are you all right? You're sweating already and I haven't even touched you."

Tyler couldn't suppress a moan. Kristin was not intentionally trying to be provocative, but Tyler's body didn't understand that fact. There was absolutely no sound other than her shallow breathing and the beat of her racing heart. She instinctively opened her legs a little wider, her mouth dry in direct contrast to the condition of the material of her undies. All she could do was nod.

Kristin cupped her calf. "Okay, here we go."

CHAPTER SEVENTEEN

B right splashes of color burst in Tyler's head. Her ears rang. She inhaled sharply, her breath caught in her throat. She arched her back, her butt starting to lift. Blackness threatened to swallow her.

The pain had returned the instant the medicated gauze touched her exposed flesh. It was all she could do not to vomit. Something Kristin was saying tried to pierce her pain. She blinked a few times and tried to focus.

"Got to do this," Tyler heard Kristin say.

"It's full of sand and probably a dozen other things I can't see."

Kristin's words were becoming clearer now. From years of intense physical therapy Tyler knew that short, staccato breaths would help get through the pain. It was what they taught in Lamaze classes to expectant mothers. Breathe and focus. She could do it. She'd done it hundreds of times. Oh, but how quickly you forget the pain and how quickly it comes barreling back to you.

Breathe and focus, breathe and focus. Tyler repeated the mantra until the pain subsided. It was still excruciating, but the threat of passing out or, worse yet, losing her lunch had passed. She opened her eyes and looked directly into Kristin's. This time they were filled with concern and sympathy and something else she didn't even try to figure out. They made her feel calm and safe.

"You're going to need stitches," Kristin said, shifting her attention back to the cut. "It's pretty deep, and even with stitches it might get infected."

"I know." Tyler's voice sounded like a croak. Breathe, focus, breathe, focus.

"It looks like we have everything we need. A needle and something called three-o silk," Kristin said, pulling out the two items.

"I don't know about that." If the pain of sewing her up was anything like the pain of cleaning her up, Tyler would throw up.

"Trust me, Tyler, it needs to be closed." Kristin's voice was firm.

Tyler looked at the cut and a new wave of nausea washed over her. From what she'd put together about her accident, she'd been unconscious when they pulled her from the ditch, and when she woke, five weeks later, her leg was bandaged. Her wound was almost completely healed by the time she saw it. But this was different. The edges of her flesh were jagged, the deep-crimson blood verifying Kristin's statement.

"I don't suppose there's some anesthesia in there?" she asked, pointing to the containers lined up neatly in the white box.

"No, but here's a vial of," Kristin hesitated as she read the fine print on the bottle, "lidocaine. Isn't that what they use to numb things, like when you get stitches?" she asked hopefully.

"Since I can't get a wireless signal out here I can't use my superior research skills to answer that question, but I have seen enough episodes of *Real Life in the ER* to say I'm pretty sure it is. However, I'm not looking forward to it," she added honestly. Tyler had developed a stubborn pain threshold, and it usually took a hefty dose of anything to dull her pain.

"And I am? I never played doctor when I was a little girl, and they eliminated home-ec the year before I would have taken it in high school. I don't watch much TV, let alone enough episodes of *Real Life in the ER*, or even *Fake Life in the ER* for that matter. Do you want me to get Paul?" Kristin asked kindly.

"Why? He can't sew any better than you can. He hates blood and would probably faint and crack his head on the only rock within miles, then you'd have two people to sew up."

"Well, at least I'd have some practice by then," Kristin said seriously.

Kristin called Paul over anyway, explained the situation, and sent him to gather some clean cloth and the flashlight. It took a few more minutes for her to assemble everything she needed while Tyler watched her closely.

She was kind of cute when she was serious, Tyler thought. Kristin furrowed her brows and scrunched her lips in concentration. Light freckles had popped out across her nose, and a few wisps of hair floated free from her ponytail.

"Ready?" Kristin asked. She wore a pair of purple rubber gloves and held a syringe in one hand, another damp square of gauze in the other. Paul stood bravely behind her holding the flashlight.

Tyler didn't say anything. No, she wasn't ready, didn't want to do this. Didn't want to faint or puke or perform any other embarrassing bodily function in front of Kristin. She had to be strong, couldn't be weak. During her rehab she had promised herself she would never be weak again.

"Do you trust me, Tyler?"

That was a double-loaded question. It wasn't a matter of trust, it was a matter of exposing herself to Kristin, and she refused to do that. She hated her weaknesses, and no way in hell would she let Kristin see them.

"Just do it." She didn't remember much after that.

❖

Dinner consisted of a small serving of fish and their normal ration of bottled water. Kristin wasn't surprised that Steven was the loudest complainer.

"If there's a waterfall of fresh water fifty feet from here, why are we still drinking only a cup of the bottled stuff? I'm thirsty."

Tyler replied. "Because we're also having the fish and don't want to introduce more than one new thing into our diet at a time. If any of us have a reaction we won't know if it's the fish or the water. The water looks fresh and tastes fresh, but it has bacteria and other stuff in it that we aren't used to, and you know what that means. I don't think any of us want that. It wouldn't be good if all of us are sick at the same time. So we introduce the fish first, see how we do with it, then the water."

She hadn't said much since Kristin stitched up her leg. Kristen suspected she was in quite a bit of pain. The cut was about three inches long and deep. Kristin had found a basic first-aid book in the kit and read the sketchy instructions on how to stitch a wound three times before she started. She could tell by Tyler's flinch when she made the first stitch that the recommended amount of lidocaine wasn't enough. She wanted to use more but Tyler refused, saying they might need it for something more critical.

Kristin did her best, keeping her stitches close and even, pulling the skin together to a slight pucker, as the picture showed. With every stick of the needle, Tyler hissed. She had stayed as still as she could, and by the time all the stitches were in, Tyler was pale and drenched in sweat. Tyler gave her a shaky thank you as Kristin covered the wound with antiseptic cream and gauze. Paul helped her to her feet and she limped to their bedroll, where she stayed until dinner.

"I've eaten fish before and never had any trouble. Give me another piece," Steven said, thrusting his plate in Kristin's direction.

"There isn't any more," Kristin replied. She was more than tired of his demands.

"What do you mean there isn't any more?" Steven looked around at his workers as if expecting to see heapings of fish on their plates.

"We only caught three," Paul answered. "And they were pretty small. By the time we gutted and skinned them, there wasn't much left." Each of them had four pieces of the fish, each about the size of a half-dollar coin.

"This isn't enough to keep a bird alive. You should have caught more."

God, Steven was an ass, Kristin thought, and told him so. "And exactly how were they supposed to do that? Tyler has stitches in her leg, her face is sunburned to a crisp, and she has blisters on her hand from trying to catch your dinner. Did you thank her?" Kristin looked around at everyone. "Did anyone?"

Kristin wasn't hungry but knew she had to eat. Before Steven had opened his mouth, she thought about giving him her share, then remembered what Tyler told her yesterday so she forced it down. God, did they crash only yesterday? It felt like much longer than that. So much had happened.

This stupid trip in the first place. Then the plane crash, starting a signal fire and keeping it lit all night, rationing their food and water, finding the waterfall, performing minor surgery on Tyler's leg. Oh, and let's not forget about discovering your desire for another woman. Forget that—how about discovering lust for another woman to the degree you never knew existed? No wonder she wasn't hungry. She was in such turmoil she wouldn't be surprised if she ran screaming into the night. Thank God Steven didn't say more or she might have.

❖

Kristin sat by the fire along with the others in their own real-life survivor group. Paul and Tyler were on a log to her right, and Paul helped Tyler to her feet. He was kind and gentle with her, like a man should be with a woman he loves. Tyler leaned heavily on him as they walked away from the fire.

When Tyler left, Kristin felt alone. Absolutely alone. What was going on with her? What had happened to make her suddenly not want her life? Hell, she didn't even know what her life was anymore. She had no outside interests, very few friends, and wasn't the woman she was five or even two years ago.

Where had that strong, self-assured woman gone? Where were the weekends spent with friends and family barbequing and drinking beer at her beach house? Where was the volunteer work she had loved to do but now did out of duty? Her house used to be filled with laughter and energy. It was alive and so was she. But not now.

Now she was living in a house that felt more like a mausoleum than a home. When was the last time she cooked in her own kitchen? When was there someone to cook for? When was there someone she wanted to cook for? When was the last time she got a little tipsy or even had one cold beer? God, her life was a mess and she had somehow let it all happen.

"A penny for your thoughts?"

Tyler's voice beside her startled Kristin. Quickly she glanced around and saw that, other than Paul, who was on watch, they were the only two still awake.

"I'm sorry, did I startle you?"

Kristin stretched her neck back and forth, trying to regain a sense of the present. "I guess I was daydreaming." Kristin had no idea how long she'd been sitting here by herself. She hadn't been aware of any of the others turning in for the night.

"In the dark?" Tyler asked. She must have looked confused because Tyler added, "Daydreaming...in the dark? It's dark? Wouldn't that be simply dreaming?"

Now Kristen felt really stupid. "Oh, yeah, I get it, sorry." She was grateful for the flames in the fire that hid her embarrassment.

"May I join you? That is, if you're not going to bed."

Say no. You don't need Tyler this close to you when you have no idea what's going on with your brain. It dangerous, way too dangerous.

"Sure, have a seat," Kristin heard herself say. It had been a long time since she played with fire. "How's the leg?" she asked once Tyler had sat down. "And don't tell me it's fine." Her pulse started racing when Tyler laughed quietly.

"Hurts like hell." Tyler looked at her. "Good enough descriptor?"

"Very good. Since I'm the doctor of record I expect to be kept informed of your progress. If I find out it's infected or you have a fever, I will not be happy."

"And I don't want to experience you not happy, do I?" Tyler asked.

Kristin smiled. "No, you don't. Trust me on that one."

They sat in silence for several minutes before Tyler responded. "That's twice now you've asked me to trust you."

Kristin thought a moment. Tyler was right, but it was more a figure of speech than a request. She told Tyler so.

Tyler turned and looked at her. Kristin didn't know which was louder, the crackling of the fire or the sizzle of tension that suddenly filled the air.

"What?" Kristin asked, not sure she wanted to know the answer to the question.

"Nothing," Tyler said, suddenly turning away.

Kristin wanted to press Tyler to explain her answer, but this time she followed her head and didn't. She changed the subject instead.

"Can I ask you something?" She felt Tyler tense beside her.

"As long as I have the right not to answer."

"Is Blake a lesbian?" Kristin asked before she lost her nerve. She had wondered about Blake's sexuality with each book. Blake didn't have sex, with men or women, in her adventures, but Kristin had detected a subtle undercurrent throughout each adventure. Or was it just her imagination?

Tyler started coughing and Kristin patted her on the back several times. "Are you okay?" She patted a few more times until Tyler shook her head.

"Sorry, guess something went down the wrong pipe."

Kristin thought that odd because she wasn't eating or drinking anything. She repeated her question. "Blake? Is she a lesbian? I mean you never really say one way or the other. You just kind of leave it to the imagination."

"And if she was?"

"That was an interesting way to answer the question," Kristin said. "I guess that's part of her allure. You never really know one way or the other. Who she sleeps with doesn't define who she is, nor does it take away from her capabilities. I guess you would have to be careful so as not to alienate your readers."

She looked at Tyler, who, even in the dim light from the fire, had a shocked look on her face. "Why so surprised? Surely you've been asked this before?"

"Actually, no."

"Come on, Tyler, you've got to be kidding? It's as plain as the words on the page."

"Is it?"

"Why are you being so evasive? I'm still going to read your next book and every other adventure Blake finds herself in, no matter who she has sex with. It doesn't matter to me."

"It doesn't?" Tyler was still only able to respond in short phrases.

"No. Actually it makes her more alluring."

"Alluring?"

"Yeah. I mean she is intelligent, articulate, good-looking, and super-capable."

"And don't forget she kicks ass."

"Definitely that. I mean she has all the classic signs of being a lesbian."

This was the last conversation Tyler was expecting when she sat down a few minutes ago. She had to admit she was curious as to where this line of questioning came from. "And a woman with all those attributes has to be a lesbian?"

Kristin furrowed her brows in the way Tyler had learned meant she was concentrating. "Of course not, but don't they?"

Tyler stepped off a cliff she wasn't aware had risen in front of her. "Do you know any lesbians?"

That concentrating expression appeared again. It was cute and Tyler's heart jumped.

"I don't think so. I must have but I just don't know it. I mean, gays and lesbians are everywhere."

"What do you think a lesbian looks like?" Okay, Tyler, *jump* off that cliff. Slowly Kristin turned her head and looked directly at her.

"Like you. Or me."

Tyler's heart stopped. Oh, shit. What in the fuck was she going to do now? Kristin was staring at her, expecting an answer. Did she say yes, you do know a lesbian? Did she tell her that she was crazy about her, wanted to take her away from Steven and all his bullshit and treat her like royalty, like she deserved?

Tyler knew she must have the classic deer-in-the-headlights look. At least her mouth wasn't hanging open. That is, she didn't think it was. But she couldn't count on anything to be what she thought it was anymore.

Thankfully Kristin said, "I mean, lesbians look like any other woman, I suppose. Some might be a little more butch than others and some might be more femme than any straight woman."

Butch? Femme? Where had she learned that?

"The whole point is that…wait a minute, what was my point?"

Beats the hell out of me. You lost me the first time you said the word lesbian.

"Oh yeah, I remember. I asked if Blake was a lesbian."

There's that word again. Quick, Logan, think of something. She's giving you that look again. The one that makes your head spin and your mouth stupid.

"I haven't decided yet." *There, I said it in a noncommittal kind of way.*

"That's pretty lame."

Okay, so much for skating around that question. Tyler returned Kristin's direct look and said with more confidence than she felt, "If she is, you'll be the first to know."

CHAPTER EIGHTEEN

K ristin?"
        Her name slowly pierced the fog of sleep. She'd been dreaming, or was she still dreaming? The voice was the same as the one that had whispered her name in the dark. Repeating it every time she kissed her, caressed her, made her come.

It had been exquisite. Every nerve in her body came alive when she touched her. Hands and fingers explored every inch of her hot flesh. Demanding and teasing lips investigated curves and damp places. Her dream lover demanded that Kristin take and receive pleasure, and Kristin greedily complied. Limbs intertwined, skin glistened, and explosions rocked the night.

"Kristin?"

There it was again. That voice that drove her wild with words, coaxed her body to respond, took her places she never knew existed. It was calling her. Calling her back, yet again to share the way only two symmetrical bodies could. Kristin reached for the voice like she had so many times in her dream. Her body lifted in anticipation of the touch, the caress, the kiss. She was ready to be taken all over again.

"Kristin." This time the voice was forceful, not seductive. A strong hand held her arms at her chest, while the other held her face. Her head shook from side to side and Kristin didn't understand what was happening. This wasn't pleasure. This wasn't erotic. This was something very different. She heard her name one last time and forced her eyes open.

Tyler hovered above her like she had so many times in her dream. But the expression on her face was not one of passion or desire. It wasn't mischievous and playful. It was cold and hard, the muscles in her jaw pulsing like a beating heart. Something was very wrong.

"Tyler?"

"Kristin, wake up. It's your turn to watch the fire."

Kristin had no idea what Tyler was talking about. Fire? What fire? The only fire she was aware of was the one that Tyler had ignited inside her.

Thankfully Tyler said more. "The signal fire. It's your shift to watch."

Comprehension dawned on Kristin like a bright light, quickly followed by apprehension. Had she said something Tyler would have heard? Did she do anything she shouldn't? Before she could answer her own question she realized Tyler had her in her grasp.

Kristin was mortified. When Tyler was waking her, it was her voice she heard. She was on the cusp of dreaming and waking, and when that voice permeated her consciousness, it drove her to dizzying heights as she reached toward it.

Tyler released her and Kristin rolled over on her side. She wanted to curl up in a fetal position and die. How could she have done such a thing? Paul was a few feet away and she was his boss's wife, making a pass, albeit a misguided one, at his girlfriend. Somebody kill me right here and now, she thought.

"Kristin?"

She jerked when Tyler touched her shoulder. Would she please just shut up and stop saying her name? "Yes, I'm up. Thanks, I've got it," she finally replied, moving to a sitting position.

"Are you okay?" Tyler asked, concern in her eyes now.

Kristin rubbed her hands over her face and noticed they were shaking. Of course they were shaking. She'd been having the most erotic dream she'd ever had with the woman kneeling in front of her. That would make anybody's hands tremble.

"Yes, I'm fine. Just a little disoriented. I'm fine, go to sleep. I've got it. I'll be fine." Kristin knew she was rambling, repeating herself, but she could barely hold herself together.

"Okay then," Tyler said. "Robert is on after you. Do not take his shift," she said sternly. "If he does nothing else, he'll take his turn on the watch. If you need anything just wake me."

Oh, she needed something all right. A swift kick in the butt, her head examined, maybe prescription medication. "I won't. Get some sleep. I'll be fine." Maybe if she said it enough times she'd convince herself. Yeah, right. That and they'd be rescued in the morning. Kristin felt ashamed when she realized she didn't want to be.

❖

Tyler thought the night would never end. Every time she closed her eyes she saw Kristin reaching for her. She had been watching her sleep when Kristin started to move. Tyler knew she was dreaming and that it was rude to watch, even if no one saw her, but she was mesmerized. Kristin's arms quivered, her legs moved back and forth slowly, her breathing turned shallow. Kristin was sensuous, her body moving unconsciously, almost without effort. When she finally settled down Tyler could only stare.

Tyler had no idea how long she had lain awake. Her brain wouldn't shut down and her body was close behind. Every time she moved, the pain in her sutured leg reminded her that Kristin had been between her legs not long ago. Kristin had touched her, spoken soothing words to her, tended to her wound. Sometime in the wee hours she fell asleep out of sheer exhaustion.

The next day Kristin went with Paul to the fishing spot. Tyler spent most of the time scouring the area around their new camp for any sign of inhabitants or anything they could use for whatever they might need it. She made several trips back and forth from the jungle to the fire pit dragging palm leaves, and additional trips with more pieces of driftwood. She managed to find what looked like very green bananas and had somehow shimmied up a tree and took a handful back to camp.

Under protest she lay in the shade that afternoon and fell asleep. She woke to the smell of fish cooking and, again under protest, was waited on by both Paul and Kristin. Steven was his obnoxious self;

Patty and Mark were constantly bickering; and Robert and Joan were barely speaking to each other. So much for "together we stand, divided we fall." If these people can't even work together for three lousy days, what would happen after thirty? Tyler didn't want to think about it.

What she did want to think about, however, was Kristin and how she seemed to have subtly changed in the last day or so. She doubted Steven or anyone else noticed, but Tyler did. She noticed everything about her. Kristin seemed to be more subdued. She never really looked at her. She avoided direct eye contact and didn't get too close. Paul had changed her dressing today, Kristin explaining how to do it step by step.

Tyler woke early two days later just as the sun was rising over the horizon. Everyone was asleep except Paul, who was on watch. She signaled to him that she was going to the water and struggled to get to her feet. She was stiff from inactivity and sore from too much activity.

She and Paul had found a hot spring not far from the waterfall. Everyone had taken a turn in the relaxing bubbles over the last few days, and a soak in it was exactly the kind of therapy Tyler needed this morning.

As quietly as she could, she moved away from the camp. Each step was agony, neither leg having the ability to give the other any rest. Finally she was at the spring. Balancing on the outcropping of rocks adjacent to it, Tyler stripped, removed her prosthesis, and slid in.

She didn't suppress a moan of pleasure as the warm water covered her body. The spring was a natural formation, and by luck or an act of God a large rock on one end could be used as a seat. She propped her stitched leg up and out of the water as best she could. From her experience with other stitches she knew the cut shouldn't get wet, at least for a few days.

The underground pressure pushed water out of a small opening in the surrounding rock, making an almost perfect Jacuzzi-type jet. Hydrotherapy had been one of the main elements of her rehabilitation, and she loved the water. She used it when she had to relearn how to balance, take weight off her stump, and unwind after a physically grueling session.

The warm water worked wonders on her sore muscles. She was able to lightly massage both her legs and lower back. Her muscles started to relax and the pain ebbed.

Getting out was more of a challenge than getting in, with half of one leg and the other not able to be fully immersed in the water. But she figured it out and even managed to climb on top of one of the rocks to dry. The morning sun had warmed it and Tyler stretched out.

She wasn't worried about anyone stumbling upon her. None of them got up before eight and, according to her watch, it was barely after six. She decided to lie there in the sun for a few minutes and enjoy the quiet, peaceful beauty around her.

Kristin held her breath and didn't move. Not that she could have, even if she wanted to. Lying in front of her, not more than ten yards away, was Tyler, completely naked. Kristin had heard her leave the camp earlier and, when she didn't immediately return, went in search of her. She'd never expected to find her like this, hands above her head, stretching to reach the sun.

Kristin didn't mean to stare but couldn't help herself. Tyler's body was perfect. She was lean, with small breasts that made her palms itch. Kristin watched the rhythmic rise and fall of her breasts for several minutes. Tyler's nipples were hard from the cool air, and Kristin had a shocking, overwhelming need to feel her tongue against them.

Tyler's stomach was flat, with an unmistakable tan line. Her thighs were muscular, the right slightly more developed than the left. Tyler shifted slightly and Kristin stopped breathing. It took more than a moment for her brain to process what her eyes were seeing. Tyler's left leg had been amputated above the knee.

Kristin stared, unable to look away. A jumble of questions ran into each other in her brain. Why didn't she tell anyone? Why didn't she tell me? Why didn't she ask for help? How was she able to climb a tree and do all the physical things she'd done for them since the crash? How did it happen? When did it happen? Was she born that way?

All of a sudden Kristin realized that was why Tyler limped and why it had become more pronounced since the crash. "Oh, my God, Tyler. I'm so sorry," Kristin said softly.

"Tyler?"

Kristin jumped at the sound of the voice. Paul was entering the clearing near where Tyler was lying. She stepped farther back into the trees.

"I thought I'd let you know everybody's starting to stir. Can't guarantee someone won't come this way. You'd better get dressed unless you want them to see your tan line."

Kristin took the opportunity of Tyler and Paul's laughter to slip away, her mind buzzing. She'd never known someone who had lost a limb, or at least didn't think she had. But she didn't know Tyler had either. Along with the standard questions of what, where, when, and how, she wondered about the more practical aspects of Tyler's life. What kind of prosthesis does she have? How does it stay on? Does it hurt? How does she take a shower? Does she wear it around the house? How does she get through the metal-detector at the airport?

Kristin entered the camp area, ignoring the others, and kept walking until she reached the water. The tide was out and she sat on the hard-packed sand. Her legs were stretched out in front of her and Kristin looked at them critically. What would she do if she lost one of them? How would she feel about herself? Would it make her stronger? Would she become self-conscious? Tyler's laughter filled the air. Kristin turned to see her laughing at something Paul had said. Kristin looked at her like she was seeing her for the first time.

Tyler was slightly shorter and thinner than Paul. She was wearing a light-blue tank top and navy khakis. Kristin studied the place where Tyler's leg should have been. There it was, a faint outline of something that wasn't her leg. It was completely unnoticeable if you didn't know it was there, but Kristin saw it now. The calf area of the pant leg was not as full as the other. The wind on the beach blew the material differently.

She walked with complete confidence and, other than the limp, showed no outward signs that she was any different from anyone else on the island. She held her head high and looked everyone in the eye when she spoke. What did make her stand out, however, was her poise and self-reliance. Had she always had it or did losing her leg make her that way?

Kristin watched Tyler as she moved through the camp smoothly and efficiently. Paul stayed nearby, occasionally helping her, as any respectable male would do. Kristin almost laughed out loud. Paul was definitely the only respectable male on the island.

She wondered about their relationship, Tyler and Paul's. What was it like to be a woman with a disability and make love? Would she feel as confident about herself when everything was exposed as she did when clothing hid all her flaws? Even women with perfect bodies were insecure and hid under the cover of darkness.

Tyler had a perfect body, Kristin thought, remembering how she looked stretched out on the rock a few minutes ago. She was thin without being skinny; lean was a better descriptor. Her arms were not only shapely but strong. Women at her gym did hundreds of crunches to get their stomachs as flat as Tyler's, and even then some resorted to the classic tummy tuck. No, Tyler had absolutely nothing to be shy about. She was a very beautiful, desirable woman.

If she and Paul weren't together before she lost her leg, how did she make love with him for the first time? Was she afraid he wouldn't find her attractive? Surely she would have told him beforehand.

Kristin suspected that Tyler was as aggressive and self-assured in bed as she was every time Kristin had seen her. Judging by the way Tyler always firmly shook her hand, the way she looked her straight in the eye, and the way she refused to be relegated to the backseat in the dinner-party conversations, there was no way she wasn't an equal in her sexual relationships. What was it like making love with Tyler Logan?

Kristin chastised herself. What business was it of hers? She had never wondered about what two people did in the privacy of their relationship. Why in heavens would she now? Natural curiosity, she supposed. Wouldn't everyone want to know the answers to these questions? If not, they weren't being honest with themselves.

❖

Three days passed before Tyler knew it. From the time she returned from the hot spring to now, tending the fire seemed to take little more than a split second. She supposed that was what life was like without the modern conveniences of a grocery store, prepackaged foods, or running water. Every minute of every day was filled with doing something to simply survive.

She glanced around her band of fellow castaways. Most were already sleeping. A few things had changed since they crashed. Mark and Robert had gathered more firewood without having to be asked, and Paul had even managed to catch a fish or two. But Joan and Patty still weren't doing anything other than the bare minimum, and Steven still bitched and berated Kristin, except more than a few times Kristin had spoken back to him. They all were disheveled, a few sunburned, and all a few pounds lighter.

The stitches on her leg were starting to itch, a good sign that her cut was healing and the risk of infection at this point was pretty low. It didn't hurt anymore but would leave a nasty scar. Like one more would really matter. At least the angle would match the one she already had.

"May I join you?"

Tyler hadn't heard anyone approach, but the crackling fire and soft sand would muffle even the noisiest treads.

Tyler was surprised that it was Kristin. They hadn't spoken more than a few words together in the past few days. Tyler missed her. Against her better judgment she replied, "Sure," and patted the sand beside her.

Kristin didn't say anything for quite a while, seeming content to watch the full moon dance over the soft waves moving toward the shore. Finally she said, "May I ask you something?"

"I suppose." Tyler hated conversations that started like this. They were always uncomfortable, especially the last one that began like this.

"Why do you limp?"

She stirred the coals and added two more logs on the fire, giving herself time to think before answering. Usually she said she had pulled a muscle or her bad knee was acting up, but for some reason she didn't want to lie to Kristin. "I had an accident."

"What happened?" Kristin's voice was soft, not at all intrusive.

"I was hit by a car." It was the first time in years Tyler had told anyone what had happened. Then again, no one had asked in years. She expected the perfunctory "I'm sorry" or "That's terrible," or whatever else people said when they heard the news. She hadn't expected Kristin's silence. It made her want to continue.

"I was training for a triathlon," Tyler paused, "you know, swim, bike, and run?" Kristin nodded. "It was a week before the race and I was running with a friend in Northern California. We hadn't seen any cars for miles and suddenly one came out of nowhere and hit me. Well, I actually don't remember anything about the run at all, but Jessica, the woman I was running with saw it happen." Still no comment or sound from Kristin.

"Jessica was on the inside, closest to the shoulder, and according to her, the car just ran right into me. She said we didn't have any warning. No horn, tires screeching, nothing. The next thing she knew I was about thirty feet in front of her, unconscious, my leg bleeding pretty badly. Because we were in such a remote area it took a while to get me to a hospital, and by then I'd lost a lot of blood from my leg. I guess it was a mess and I was covered with road rash. Again, according to Jessica and the doctors that treated me.

"I was in the hospital for months and in a coma for the first few weeks. They tried to save my leg but it was too damaged. By the time I woke up, it was gone, along with my spleen and some intestines." She didn't mention that infection had almost killed her.

"When did it happen?"

"Five years ago." Some days it seemed like yesterday. Her family knew, of course, as did Paul, her therapists, and doctors. Occasionally when she wore shorts, someone, invariably a child, would ask, "Hey, lady, what happened to your leg?" She didn't mind. Children were always completely honest and innocently curious. Her answer, much to the delight of the child, was always the same—"Shark." She didn't allow anyone to get close enough to seriously ask.

"Were you and Paul together then?"

"Sort of," she answered evasively. "We were always close, and he was one of the first people I saw when I woke up from the surgery. He stayed with me for weeks, helping me through it." It was more like months he slept in the chair beside her bed.

"I can see how love can grow as a result of something like that."

Or die, Tyler thought.

"I have a cousin who says before you marry someone you should go through every season, a vacation, and preferably a major illness. If you can get through all of that, you'll probably last forever." Kristin resumed shifting sand through her fingers.

"He's definitely got a point," Tyler replied. Her relationship with Jessica lasted through two of the three.

"Did they ever find the guy, the one that ran into you?"

"No. All Jessica could tell the police was that the car was a dark color—blue, maybe black. It happened so fast she didn't see anything else, and after I was hit she was focused on me, not the car." Tyler had often wondered what she would do if the driver was ever caught. Would she feel a sense of closure, relief, revenge, justice? She had no idea and, after the first few years, had actually stopped thinking about it. She'd moved on.

"What about your friend? The one running with you?"

Tyler hesitated before answering. What should she say about Jessica? That she was cowardly, insensitive, and selfish? That she did more to hurt Tyler than the accident and subsequent rehab ever could? She settled for, "She was understandably a little rattled. She had some problems but I guess she's okay now. I don't see her anymore."

"I don't know what I'm supposed to say," Kristin admitted. "'I'm sorry' sounds trite and superficial, but I am sorry it happened to you."

"Thanks, but you don't have to say anything. It happened, and through the skill of many talented people I survived. And now five years later here I am stranded on a desert island. If it's not one thing it's another, isn't it?" Tyler tried to lighten the conversation.

"I suppose it is, but most people rarely experience one life-altering event. You're on your second."

Tyler faced Kristin for the first time since their conversation began. "It certainly puts life into perspective, doesn't it?"

Kristin held her gaze for several seconds before turning to watch the sand slide from between her fingers. "Yes, it certainly does."

❖

The moon was high in the sky when Kristin finally spoke again. "Have you given any more thought to Blake's situation?"

Tyler turned and looked at her. "Situation?"

"Yeah, you know. If she comes out as a lesbian?"

Tyler was hoping Kristin wouldn't pick up their earlier conversation about Blake's sexual orientation, and she certainly didn't expect it now. Something about Kristin made her say things she normally didn't. At this rate she would tell Kristen that she too was a lesbian and confess her desire to do more than talk about being one. She wanted to demonstrate. And she wanted to demonstrate with Kristin. She did not want to have this conversation.

"I've been a little busy."

"I know, but you haven't even thought about it?"

Tyler heard the question in her voice. "Nope, sorry. Ask me about fish, what fruit is on the bushes surrounding the camp, I can answer that." Tyler hoped that response would change the subject.

"Want to flush it out now?"

Hope was obviously not a good strategy. "Not really." Actually no. More specifically, HELL NO.

"Are any of your characters based on real people?"

Tyler grabbed onto the change of subject. "My friends sometimes think so but, no, they're not modeled on anyone. Actually Blake is more like what I'd like to be. She always knows what to say, when to say it, and can do anything. She always lands on her feet. Whenever I'm in a tough spot I just think, 'What would Blake do?'"

"How do you write? I mean, I'm sure everyone asks that question. Where do you get your ideas?"

"It just happens. Everyone's different. Some writers plot out every scene, some just sit down and see what comes out. I know an author who can only write if he's in the same place, at the same time, with the same computer, and wearing the same pair of shoes. Others can do it anywhere, any time."

"Which are you?"

Tyler had answered this question hundreds of times, but when Kristin asked it was like hearing it the very first time. "I'm kind of in the middle, I guess. I don't need a lot of structure. Ideas for scenes come to me in the oddest places sometimes. I usually have a pen and paper with me all the time. You never know if a scene or the perfect dialogue will come to you while getting a pedicure or in the bread aisle of the grocery store."

Kristin laughed and suddenly Tyler was very warm. She shifted away from the fire a little, trying to convince herself that was the cause, not the sound of Kristin's laugh.

"Where was the oddest place you've been inspired?" Kristin laughed. "Is that even a proper sentence—the oddest place you've been inspired?"

Tyler laughed with her. "I don't know. That's what I have an editor for. I just write it, she makes it readable." Tyler thought about Roberta and how she would want to leverage the crash into another Blake Hudson adventure, or maybe two or three.

Tyler leaned back and stretched her arms out behind her. "It's not really unusual, but quite a few ideas came to me when I was doing physical therapy. The pain was so intense I just went somewhere else in my head, I guess. Some of what I consider my best scenes in book three and four came from those grueling sessions." She'd never told anyone that fact. Her standard reply, like the shark answer, was more lie than truth. She was intensely private about her writing, and even Paul and Roberta didn't know about some aspects of it. But Kristin did.

Kristin didn't say anything for a moment. "I can't even imagine," she finally said quietly. Her statement wasn't sympathetic, patronizing, or pitying. It was simply a fact.

"I hope you or somebody you love never does."

"Do you have to, I mean are you still...hell, I don't know how to ask, but do you have therapy now?"

Tyler didn't mind the question or the awkward way Kristin asked it. She was at least honest about not knowing the exact, proper words to use. Since the accident too many people had tiptoed around the subject. Good God, she was missing a leg—talk about the elephant in the room.

"No. I have to go in once in a while to get the prosthesis checked. Kind of like a fifty-thousand-mile checkup. Usually it's just tweak here or an adjustment there. Nothing major, at least not during the last few years."

"How are you doing? I mean now, here in the sand and everything?"

Tyler appreciated Kristin's honest questions. "Well, it is a lot easier to walk on solid ground without miniscule particles of sand getting in it. I'm not sure what the salt water will do to it, but I'll find out in a few more days, I'm sure."

"You were going to tell me about where you write," Kristin said.

Tyler silently thanked her for changing the subject again. Things were getting too serious. "I used to be able to write anywhere. On a bus, in a park, or in the middle of a shopping mall. Anyplace I had a pen and something to write on. I remember one time I was at a baseball game between the Yankees and the Mets. Huge crosstown rivalry. Sixty thousand New York half-drunk fans yelling, screaming, and generally talking smack about the other team," Tyler said, reminiscing. "It was the bottom of the eighth inning, the score was tied, and all of a sudden I had to get my thoughts on paper. I borrowed a pen from the guy in front of me, and before the game was over I'd filled up every bit of white space on his program, mine, and about half a dozen others. I think it ended up being close to ten thousand words. Everybody around me thought I was nuts." Tyler looked at Kristin and couldn't help but smile. "I thought I was nuts, but it was as if I couldn't stop. It just kept coming and coming, and I knew if I didn't get it down right then and there, I'd lose it forever. And it was pretty good stuff, if I say so myself."

"What was it? I've read all of Blake's adventures, more than once, I'm not embarrassed to say."

Tyler stared to answer but Kristin put a hand up, stopping her. "No," Kristin said. "Don't tell me, give me a clue."

"A clue?"

"No, I've got something even better. I bet I can tell you the book and the scene in, hmm," Kristin said, putting her hand under her chin and contemplating, "ten yes-or-no questions. Yep," she said confidently, "I bet I can guess it in ten questions."

Tyler had never seen this side of Kristin. She was confident, playful, and thought-provoking. Quite alluring. She accepted the challenge. "And what if you don't?"

Even in the firelight Tyler could see the wheels turning behind Kristin's eyes. The wheels stopped an instant before Tyler stopped breathing. Kristin was looking at her with anything but playfulness now. "I'll do anything you want."

Another log split and the fire flared, but it was nothing compared to what was happening inside Tyler. Her blood was hot, racing through her veins from the top of her head to the tip of her toes. She was breathing too fast, making her light-headed, and if she were standing her knees would surely buckle.

Kristin continued to look at her, her eyes never wavering. They were direct, confident, and without a doubt she was dead serious.

"And if you do?" Tyler managed to strangle out.

"Then you do anything I want."

Kristin watched the emotions swirl in Tyler's eyes as she waited for her answer. When she sat down she hadn't intended for the conversation to take this turn. Actually she had no clue what they were going to talk about or what she was going to say, and she certainly had no idea she was going to practically proposition Tyler. But she hadn't been herself since seeing Tyler naked on the rock.

She was surprised that Tyler or Paul hadn't heard her stumble away from the hot spring. She'd made enough noise, for crying out loud. Her reaction to seeing Tyler had stunned her. Not discovering the situation with her leg but her body's reaction to Tyler's nude form. Her heart beat faster, her hands shook, and her groin started to throb. She was aroused at the sight of Tyler, her breasts rising and falling with each breath, her arms over her head making her body long and angular. Kristin wanted to run her hands over every line and curve and dip into the dark curly hair between Tyler's legs. She wanted to do it then and she wanted to do it now.

"Do we have a deal?" Kristin asked, suddenly afraid Tyler would run.

Tyler visibly swallowed before answering. "Yes." That three-letter word was more than a simple answer.

"You're not going to cheat on me, are you? Change the scene or anything," Kristin asked breathlessly.

"I'd never cheat on you, Kristin."

No, you wouldn't, Kristin thought. She didn't know how, but she was certain Tyler was telling the truth.

Kristin had ten questions. She asked each one carefully, one building on the other. By the eighth question, Kristin knew the answer. The ninth question confirmed it. The tenth and final question sealed it. Kristin calmly recited the name of the book and the scene.

"I guess you won."

"I guess I did."

"I guess this makes you my biggest fan."

"I guess it does."

"I guess I have to pay up."

"I know you do."

"And just what is it you want me to do?"

Tension and anticipation was as thick as the black sky overhead. Her stomach was in knots. She knew and Tyler knew she knew. Yet she waited. Waited and watched Tyler. She waited for any sign from Tyler. Finally she said, "Kiss me."

CHAPTER NINETEEN

The entire world stopped. The fire stopped crackling, the waves no longer crashed against the rocks, and everybody on the face of the earth no longer existed. Nothing existed except the bill presented to her from the beautiful woman in front of her.

Tyler knew she'd heard Kristin correctly. She had no doubt about the payment due Kristin. She had made a bet and always honored a commitment, however absolutely out of her mind she must have been when she made it.

Her mouth was dry, and she was completely incapable of coherent thought. Her body was doing the talking for her, telling her to bend her head, just a little. Whispering to her to shift her gaze from the desire burning in Kristin's eyes to her open, wet, waiting lips commanding Tyler to kiss her.

"We shouldn't do this," Tyler managed to say.

"Why not?" Kristin was watching Tyler's mouth move.

"Dozens of reasons."

"Name three."

Kristin moved closer and Tyler felt her warm breath on her face. "Steven."

"One."

"It will cause major problems."

"Two."

"You're not a lesbian." Even to Tyler her words sounded like a big fat lie. Kristin was inches from her, eyes burning, lips wet with desire.

"Then why do I want you to kiss me?"

Tyler gave up, gave in, or whatever words she could think of to justify kissing Kristin. She didn't care. She wanted to kiss her. She'd wanted to do just that for days, even longer than that, she finally admitted.

"Kristin," Tyler said, a moment of sanity returning. Kristin put two soft fingers on her lips, silencing her protests. But Tyler didn't really know what she would have said anyway, because she wanted to kiss her. Desperately. Right now, at this moment, if she had to choose between kissing Kristin and being rescued from this stupid island, she'd pick the kiss. Tyler quit fighting and rationalizing and kissed her.

Soft. Tender. Perfect. Those and many other equally descriptive words floated around the fringes of Kristin's consciousness. Kristin's world completely shifted. She thought she knew what passion was. She thought she knew desire. She thought she had experienced everything her body was capable of. Until her lips met Tyler's.

She absolutely came alive. Every nerve tingled and every sense shifted into full overdrive. A fog she hadn't known surrounded her lifted. She felt the ocean breeze on her face, the warmth from the fire on her back, the soft rolling waves in the distance.

Her hands trembled when she cupped Tyler's cheek. Her skin was soft, her jaw strong, and Kristin felt each muscle move as Tyler kissed her. Kristin envisioned their two silhouettes in the firelight and was hungry for more than just Tyler's kisses. She slid her hand behind Tyler's head, fully intending to deepen the kiss.

"Are you two fucking crazy?"

Kristin jerked back as if she'd been burned by the coals behind her. Paul was standing between her, Tyler, and the fire. Tyler scrambled to her feet.

Oh, my God, what did we do, Kristin asked herself. She had totally forgotten about Paul. She wasn't in love with Steven, hadn't been for several years, but there was Paul. Tyler and Paul.

"Paul," Tyler said.

"Don't 'Paul' me, Tyler." Paul said through clenched teeth.

"It's my fault." Kristin began to get to her feet. "I'm sorry, Paul. I never should have—"

"Have you lost your mind, Tyler? Anybody could see you two. Jesus, I thought you had more sense than that."

Kristin looked back and forth between Tyler and Paul. What was going on? He should be furious, not chastising his girlfriend for kissing someone in public. Were they into three-ways? Oh, God, no. How could she have been so wrong? Suddenly she needed to vomit. She turned and ran to the trees.

❖

Paul grabbed Tyler's arm, stopping her from following Kristin. She heard her retching and wanted to go to her.

"Don't," Paul said.

"Fuck." Tyler rubbed her hands over her face.

"If I hadn't waked up when I did, you certainly would have been. What's going on?" Paul pulled her farther away from the fire and the prying ears of the others.

"I don't know, it just happened." She knew her answer was lame when Paul snorted.

"Please, Tyler. Don't give me that crap and don't bullshit yourself. That was not 'just happening.'"

"I don't know," Tyler said, more forceful this time. "One minute we were talking about writing, and the next she told me to kiss her."

"She *told* you to kiss her?"

Tyler explained the course of events leading up to the kiss that had rocked her to her soul. As she talked she felt like she'd observed the entire event.

"Holy crap," Paul said.

"What am I going to do?" Tyler had absolutely no idea what was next. She had never experienced a situation like this and had no frame of reference.

"You're asking me? You're the one that kissed her."

"You invited me on this stupid trip. If you were out of the closet I wouldn't be kissing your boss's wife." That statement made absolutely no sense and Tyler ran her fingers through her short hair, pulling it hard enough to cause pain, hoping to knock some sense into her. "God, what a fucking soap opera."

Paul answered as if he hadn't heard her. "If it makes you feel any better, I don't think anybody else saw you."

"And that should make me feel better?" Actually it did, but that wasn't her biggest problem at this point.

"That should be a relief. I was watching you for at least ten minutes, and it was clear to me that something was going on."

"These people are so clueless." Like that made it right?

"Well, you'll be lucky if Steven doesn't punch you in the mouth. And fire me," Paul said, not quiet enough for Tyler not to hear.

"I'm sorry, Paul. You know I'd never do anything to jeopardize your job." Now she really was starting to worry, but for very different reasons. She could take care of herself and would take responsibility for her actions, but Paul would get caught in the crossfire if she didn't... Didn't what? Kiss Kristin again? God knew she wanted to. She'd caved once and it would be easier to rationalize a second time.

"Don't worry about it. You need to figure out what to do. Has it occurred to you that Kristin might be wondering why you kissed her?"

Tyler stopped walking and stared at Paul like he'd just revealed the six matching numbers the day before the lottery.

"She told you to kiss her, Tyler. If you were straight you wouldn't have done it even if a desirable woman like Kristin asked you. That," Paul said, poking her with his finger, "is your problem."

Paul returned to the fire, leaving Tyler by herself, her jumbled thoughts making her dizzy. She dropped to the sand and lay on her back, covering her face with her hands. She remembered doing that as a child when she was frightened. In her young mind if she couldn't see the scary thing, then it wasn't really there. But she was a grown-up now. How did her life go from fabulous to shit in only seven days?

CHAPTER TWENTY

Paul's statement resounded in Kristin's brain like a broken record. "Anybody could see you two. Jesus, Tyler, I thought you had more sense than that." Every time it ran through her head Kristin wanted to retch—again. She had thrown up her dinner and what felt like her entire insides. No way could she sleep so she didn't even try.

She walked along the shoreline for hours. She stayed in sight of the fire but didn't really care if the darkness swallowed her. What was she thinking? What had gotten into her? Jesus, she'd made a pass at someone—and a woman at that? And it would have been a threesome. When would she have discovered that—when more than two hands caressed her? Could it get any more bizarre than this?

"Stop it, Kristin," she said into the wind. "You knew exactly what you were doing, and you wanted to do it, so stop acting like something swooped in and took over your will. For the first time in a very long time you actually did something." The water covered her feet and ankles as she walked. It was cool and refreshing. "And it was the stupidest thing I've ever done."

Kristin was still awake when the sun finally rose. She had walked most of the night, and when exhaustion drove her back to camp she lay down on her bedroll and watched the sky overhead. Shooting stars had danced across the night sky, their heat leaving white trails in their wake. The flashes in the sky mimicked her racing thoughts. One minute she was confident about who she was and what she wanted, the next, completely clueless.

Giving up on sleep, Kristin sat up and couldn't keep from looking in the direction where Tyler and Paul slept. She expected to see Tyler sleeping but instead looked directly into clear, dark eyes. Her pulse sped up and nausea gripped her by the throat.

She wasn't ready to face Tyler. She was certainly not ready to face Paul. She'd made a pass at his girlfriend, for God's sake. She wasn't any better than any of the lecherous men Steven associated with. She felt sick to her stomach—again. It was one thing to discover after almost ten years of dating and eight years of marriage that she might be a lesbian. But to experiment on the girlfriend of one of her husband's closest advisors was absolute stupidity.

Somehow Kristin managed to avoid Tyler for most of the day, but just before the sun set behind the tall trees her luck ran out.

"Kristin," Tyler said from behind her. She had been stripping the leaves off the branches they would use for their signal fire that night.

"I want to apologize," Kristin blurted out, her voice more steady than she felt.

"Kristin."

"No, please, just let me—"

"What do you think you need to apologize for?"

"Kissing you."

"Technically you asked me to kiss *you*."

"Then I'm even sorrier for putting you in that position."

"Why?"

"I beg your pardon?" She wasn't expecting Tyler's question and finally turned and looked at her. Tyler was breathtaking. Kristin's heart skipped and an entire colony of butterflies woke up in her stomach.

"Why are you sorry? You seemed to have wanted it at the time. What changed your mind?"

Tyler's voice didn't sound angry or condescending. It sounded calm, asking what appeared to be a simple question. "Lots of things."

"Name three."

Kristin remembered their conversation just before they kissed when she had said basically the same thing to Tyler.

"Paul."

"One."

"It will cause problems." Tyler had said the same thing.

"Two."

"You're not a lesbian." This conversation was surreal.

"Then why *did* I kiss you?"

"I don't know." Kristin ran her hands through her hair. "Afraid to piss off the boss's wife?"

Tyler chuckled and looked at her in disbelief. "Do you really think *that* would stop me from doing something?"

She was confused. This discussion wasn't going the way she wanted. But she hadn't planned on even having a conversation with Tyler. Even though she knew it would be impossible, she hoped she wouldn't have to face Tyler ever again. So much for wishful thinking.

"Have you ever kissed a woman?" Tyler asked, again throwing her a curve.

Kristin didn't know how to answer but recalled Grace Howard in the tenth grade on the couch in her basement. But that had been only a peck or two. Two teenagers simply giggling and tickling each other. Kristin often wondered what would have happened if her father hadn't come barreling down the stairs looking for his glasses.

"You don't have to answer that." Tyler was looking at her as if she were reading her mind. "Do you think I would have kissed you if I didn't want to?"

That thought had caused her sleeplessness the night before. Before last night, if a woman had said to her what Kristin had said to Tyler, would she have kissed her? Of course not. Other than the last few days she'd never even considered kissing another woman. Kristin wanted to erase the last week, but was equally afraid this was nothing but a bad dream and she'd wake up alone.

Tyler was looking at her, expecting an answer. Her eyes were piercing, her brow furrowed. Kristin wanted to smooth away the lines and let her fingers explore the rest of Tyler's face. It felt so good the first time.

"Kristin!" Steven hollered, his voice breaking through the still evening air. "Kristin, where are you? I'm hungry. I need something to eat." When Kristin didn't immediately answer, Steven repeated his demand.

"You'd better go," Tyler said, breaking eye contact.

Chapter Twenty-one

Y ou'd better figure out what you're going to do, Tyler."
Paul was sitting next to her on a large tree stump, sipping his morning ration of coffee. He hadn't shaved since the crash and looked rather dashing in his week-old stubble.

"I'm not going to *do* anything," Tyler replied.

"Then you'd better come to grips with whatever you're dealing with because the sparks flying between you and Kristin are going to cause one or both of you to spontaneously combust."

"Shut up, Paul," Tyler said, much more snippy than he deserved. She hadn't slept well the last few nights, she had a major headache that could very easily turn into a migraine, and she didn't even want to think about how much her leg hurt. All this before nine in the morning was more than she could take, so she took it out on him instead.

"Don't bite my head off, I'm the best friend, remember," he said, holding up his free hand and pointing at her. "Something's going on between you two and pretty soon even those thick-headed heteros are going to figure it out." Paul was no longer pointing at her but at the others gathered around the morning fire. "Especially Steven."

That got her attention. "What do you mean?"

"I mean he watches Kristin like a hawk, and since you and Kristin have become inseparable, he's going to put two and two together."

"There's nothing going on, Paul."

He finished the liquid in his cup before replying. "Then something had better be because you're pulled tighter than a piano wire. I've seen you at work, Tyler, and you've never been like this."

"What do you mean, you've seen me at work?"

"With women. I've watched you when you're on the prowl."

"On the prowl? I do not prowl." Tyler lost interest in her weak cup of coffee.

"Yes, Tyler, you do. When you need to get laid you're like a jungle cat stalking her prey. I've seen you. We've been in the same bars, parties, or wherever young, hip homosexuals congregate. Trust me, sister, you're on the prowl."

"I am *not* on the prowl, and certainly not with your boss's wife. How stupid would that be? We're trying to stay alive here," Tyler said, both palms up. "Just when do you think I have time to think about sex?"

"Whenever Kristin's within a hundred yards. When you're tossing and turning all night, every minute you're awake because you're thinking of her. Do you want me to continue? Because you know I can."

"Shut up," Tyler said again. Paul was right but Tyler was too tired to fight anymore. "Why in the hell did I pick you for my best friend?"

"Because I'm handsome, charming, and play a mean game of poker."

Tyler couldn't help but smile, the conversation taking a lighter tone. "You mean lose at poker."

"That was strip poker, and you have to admit we had a hell of a good time, didn't we?"

Tyler remembered the game he was referring to. Before she met Jessica she and Paul were double-dating and Paul had volunteered to cook for the four of them. After three bottles of wine his date suggested a friendly game of strip poker. Needless to say, before the night was over, clothes were scattered around the room and Paul and his George Clooney look-alike date disappeared into his bedroom and didn't reappear until after Tyler's date had gone home the next morning.

"God, we were young," Tyler replied nostalgically. "And incredibly stupid."

"Don't forget about pretty damn lucky." Both of them had had more than a few lovers and, so far, didn't have any lifelong medical conditions as a result.

"So what's really going on, Tyler?" Paul's voice had softened and he was back to serious now.

"I don't know." She sighed. "I don't know. I shouldn't, but I think about her all the time. I want to be close to her, help her, save her from that asshole Steven. I just want to be with her. I haven't wanted to just be with someone since the accident. And Kristin definitely doesn't know what she wants. She asked me to kiss her then apologized for doing so. That's why straight women are on my do-not-touch list. They mess with your mind." Tyler rubbed her hands over her sunburned face. "I'm an emotional wreck."

Tyler expected Paul to press her more, but instead he scampered to his feet and held out his hand. "Come on. Let's get out of earshot of these people. How about a walk?"

He was right. They shouldn't be having this conversation with everyone so close. Maybe a change of scenery and not constantly watching for Kristin to appear would clear her mind. Yeah, right. And they'd discover pirate gold on this stupid island.

Paul easily pulled Tyler to her feet and led her in the direction of the pond, then hung the white hand towel on the first tree along the path. They all had begun to notify the others like this when someone was going to take a bath. It reminded her of the way her roommate would leave a necktie on the front door of their apartment when she was entertaining, as she called it. So Tyler wasn't surprised if she encountered a strange man in the bathroom or their tiny kitchen. Was she ever glad that time in her life was over.

They settled comfortably on the large boulder that Tyler always lay on after a dip to let the sun dry her body. Paul didn't say anything. He didn't have to. He would sit here all day if he had to until she opened up. She talked when she was ready, not on anyone else's timetable. Before Kristin, Paul was the only person she had ever talked to about life, love, her dreams, failures, and her fears about life as an amputee. He was more than her best friend—he was the sister she'd lost and the counselor she'd never go to.

"I don't know what to do." Tyler was ready to talk.

"So you said."

"I know I keep repeating myself, but I don't know what else to say. And isn't that pitiful? I can crank out a hundred thousand words practically without blinking an eye, and in this case I can't even form a complete thought, let alone a coherent sentence. We're under some hellacious stress here in our little paradise, and stress makes people do things they might not normally do."

"Do you honestly believe that?"

Was she just repeating something she'd heard or read about somewhere? "Actually, I'm not sure, but I do know it's not true with me. Or at least I thought it wasn't true." Everything about her life had changed on this trip and she was in completely unfamiliar territory. And she hated being in that position.

"So what's the problem?"

"I'm acting so out of character. With Kristin."

"Like what?"

"I told her about the accident."

"Wow," Paul replied, half word, half sound. "You've never told anyone."

"I know, and the funny thing is, it was really easy. She asked why I had a limp and I told her. Just like that." Tyler snapped her fingers. "Everything. And I mean everything."

"What did she say?" Paul asked hesitantly.

He was apparently trying hard not to pepper her with questions or slap her on the back with congratulations. He'd never understood why she kept the accident a secret, but respected her wishes nonetheless.

"She didn't really say anything. I mean, no empty words of sympathy, no platitudes, no sign of morbid curiosity." Tyler had experienced all of those and more. "She simply asked if you and I were together at the time, commented about how something like that could make love stronger. She said that most people rarely experience one life-altering event and that I was on my second."

The conversation had been so pivotal Tyler could recite every word if asked.

"Kristin is a very insightful woman."

"Then maybe she can figure out why I want to do more than kiss her. Why I want to see her naked, lying on this rock waiting for me. Why I want her to touch me, *really* touch me, not be just another anonymous hand groping in my pants. I want to lie in the sun with her, taste the salt on her skin, make her scream my name in the blazing light of day. I want to talk with her about everything, and nothing at all. I want to debate politics and baseball, and critique the latest bestseller with her. I want to know her dreams. I want to be a part of those dreams."

"Then do it."

Tyler chuckled. "Yeah, right." If it were only that simple, that uncomplicated. What would she have done if she'd met Kristin in a coffee shop or at the bookstore. If she wasn't the wife of Paul's boss.

"Why not?"

"I don't have any answers."

"Maybe that's because there really aren't any questions." Paul stood and walked away, leaving Tyler alone with her thoughts.

❖

"It's Tyler and Paul," Joan said as Kristin stared at the white cloth blowing lightly in the breeze. "They've been gone a long time," she added before walking away.

Kristin's stomach lurched and she was afraid she'd throw up the miniscule amount of breakfast she'd managed to choke down. Tyler and Paul? Alone at the pond? Does that mean what I think it means? Have they gone away for some conjugal reconnection?

God, what in the hell was going on? One minute she and Tyler were business acquaintances, the next she was practically begging Tyler to kiss her. Then when she apologized for putting Tyler in that position, Tyler hinted that their kiss was perfectly normal. Actually she had done more than hint; she had practically told her outright that she had not been averse to kissing Kristin.

She slumped down onto the sand at the base of the "signal" tree. She was tired, emotionally wrung out, and had no idea what was happening to her.

"She's at the pond," a voice said from above her. Kristin looked up. Shielding her eyes from the sun's rays, all she could see was a silhouette. It looked like Paul. The shadow moved, slightly blocking out the sun and giving Kristin her first glimpse of him that day.

"I beg your pardon?"

"Tyler, she's at the pond," he said again.

Kristin wasn't sure if his statement was just that or something else. But what else could it be? The longer he stood in front of her the clearer his meaning became.

Kristin got to her feet. "But you…"

"She's my best friend. Nothing more," Paul said quietly, almost reverently. "And because I'm *her* best friend she's here, stuck on this island with the rest of this pathetic group instead of back in San Francisco living her life and churning out another Blake Hudson adventure."

Kristin was speechless. It would never have occurred to her that Tyler and Paul were anything other than a couple. They had an aura around them of two people who loved each other. That connection, the way they practically finished each other's sentences and knew exactly what the other was thinking even before they did.

And they're just friends? Then that makes Tyler…

CHAPTER TWENTY-TWO

Tyler felt weightless in the cool water. Back and forth she swam across the large pool created at the base of the waterfall. It felt good to release some of the stress and anxiety she'd kept bottled up over the past several days. Who would blame her? A week ago she was in her penthouse apartment finishing a book for which she had already received an advance of one million dollars. And that was just the down payment. Her publisher had assured her that Blake Hudson's latest adventure would pay both of them handsomely.

And now look at her. She had survived a plane crash, set up a make-shift camp, built a signal fire, learned how to spear fish, had stitches put into her leg with not nearly enough numbing medicine, and kissed the boss's wife. All in all, not a bad week. It certainly wasn't the mundane day-in, day-out life she was used to. But she certainly hadn't expected this. These kinds of things only happened in good fiction. And thank God she wrote well-researched fiction. Where would they be if she hadn't known what to do? In a hell of a lot worse situation.

Tyler stopped swimming and ducked under the waterfall. It was cooler here than out in the direct sunlight, and she couldn't see through the heavy water falling from the craggy rocks above her head. If she couldn't see out, no one could see in.

She ran her hands over her body, lightly skimming her sensitive parts. She was on edge from being near Kristin and it wouldn't take much for her to climax. But she didn't want to come thinking of Kristin, imagining her lips kissing her, her hands on her, Kristin's fingers in her. Since nothing other than the real thing would be enough, she gritted her teeth and pushed the desire to the back of her mind.

Her bath complete, Tyler moved forward, rinsing her short hair under the water. Moving until the water was at her waist, she wiped her face with her hands and froze. Kristin was walking toward the pond.

❖

As Kristin moved closer, she started to disrobe and Tyler's heart raced in time to her breathing. Kristin's fingers quickly unbuttoned her shirt, letting it fall off her shoulders into the sand behind her. She reached around behind her back and the lacy blue bra fell away next.

Kristin was beautiful. Her breasts were small and perfect, and Tyler couldn't take her eyes off them. She wanted to touch them, run her fingers over what looked like very soft skin, and tease the pale-pink nipples into hardness.

Tyler's stomach jumped when Kristin's hands dropped to her waist and, with complete deliberateness, unsnapped her shorts. She couldn't help but stare as she watched the zipper making a lazy trail downward.

Tyler's pulse hammered in her head. She had seen women strip before, some much more provocative than this, but none had elicited the response in her body like she was having now. Without hesitation Kristin stepped out of the last remaining clothing and Tyler was riveted as Kristin, naked, closed the distance between them.

Kristin entered the water, the calm ripples mimicking her smooth, deliberate movements. She was stunning, her skin flawless without a visible freckle or blemish, only a faint line disclosing the modesty of her swimsuit.

Tyler expected Kristin to stop but she didn't until her arms were around her neck, their lips touching. Passion and desire exploded inside but Tyler held back. She'd had women in this position before,

well, not exactly in *this* position, but naked and in her arms, t
for sure, where tongues, hands, fingers, and lips would fin
way into warm, dark places. Hot breath and sweat would till the
air around them. Sighs, moans, and screams would penetrate the
silence until no sound was left except the dull beating of her heart.
But this was the first time since the accident that Tyler had been
equally naked—and vulnerable.

As she kissed her, Kristin's hands dropped from around her
neck and trailed down her back, pulling Tyler closer. Tyler's hard
nipples pressed against Kristin's as their bodies fit perfectly together.
Kristin grabbed her ass and pulled her even closer, sliding a thigh
between Tyler's legs.

Tyler was incapable of thought and instinct took over. She
returned Kristin's kisses passionately, then softly, then passionately
again. Her lips were softer than Tyler remembered and more
demanding than she ever thought she would experience. Kristin
opened her mouth and Tyler slipped her tongue inside.

Kristin's breath was hot in her mouth, her hands strong and
confident on her body. Tyler had never been as aroused as she was
with Kristin in her arms. Her insides were like molten lava, flowing
on their own course throughout her body. Every place Kristin
touched her made Tyler's skin sizzle with sensation. She was dizzy
as waves of desire surged through her. Tyler needed Kristin and she
needed her now.

Sliding back into the water and behind the waterfall, she
turned and pinned Kristin against the smooth rock. It was her turn
to explore. She dragged her mouth from Kristin's and kissed her
neck, starting from under her chin to her collarbone and back again.
She didn't keep track of how many times she was pulled back to the
temptation of Kristin's hot mouth.

Tyler closed her hands over Kristin's breast, her fingers
lightly brushing her nipple. Kristin gasped and pulled Tyler closer,
effectively trapping her hand between them, ending any further
exploration. Tyler needed to feel Kristin, touch her, taste her. She
pulled back, giving her enough room to lower her head and at the
same time lifting Kristin out of the water, exposing her breasts.

"You are so beautiful," Tyler said in awe, as she looked at Kristin. Tyler traced the tan line with her tongue. Kristin rubbed against her thigh when Tyler circled the nipple. When she closed her lips over it, Kristin moaned. Tyler worshiped one breast then the other, trailing kisses up and down the slight curve. When she hesitated over the tight nipple, Kristin raised up, effectively begging her to suck it.

Never leaving her breasts, Tyler skimmed one hand down the center of Kristin's stomach, stopping just above her pubic bone. She kept it there for a few moments until detecting Kristin's subtle signal for her to move farther.

Warm softness greeted her fingers as she gently explored Kristin's center, one finger poised at the entrance as if asking permission.

When Kristin softly murmured yes, Tyler completely lost control. Kristin was warm and wet, drawing her in even more.

"More," Kristin said, her head back as far as the wall would allow.

A second finger accompanied the first and Kristin inhaled sharply. Tyler stopped, frozen with fear that she had hurt her.

"No," Kristin pleaded. "Don't stop."

Kristin grabbed Tyler's wrist with strength she didn't expect and guided Tyler's fingers even deeper. Tyler caressed Kristin's clit with her thumb and Kristin tightened around her. Kristin's breath quickened. Tyler knew Kristin was rising to orgasm, and as much as she wanted to savor every moment, she wanted to experience Kristin coming in her arms even more. She slid her fingers in and out, faster with each stroke. Kristin was panting now, her breath coming in short, shallow bursts. Kristin tightened around her fingers even more, then froze for a split second.

Spasms rocked Kristin as her orgasm rocketed through her. Her insides pulsed around Tyler's fingers and her clit twitched under Tyler's caress. Waves rocked her body as flashes of bright light blinded her. Her toes curled, her heart hammered, and she erupted again. Three, then four more times she came, each harder and more intense than the last. Tyler held her tight as she rode the waves of orgasm over and over. Tyler was strong yet gentle with her. Finally, when she was too sensitive to take any more, she stilled Tyler's hand.

Kristin didn't know how long she stayed that way—with Tyler's arm around her, her fingers deep inside. All Kristin knew or even cared about was how good she felt and how much she wanted this to go on forever.

Sometime during the raging climax her head had fallen on Tyler's shoulder. Mustering up her strength, Kristin lifted her head and opened her eyes. Tyler was looking at her with a mix of tenderness, concern, and uncertainty. Kristin didn't know what to say. Words couldn't explain how Tyler had made her come alive, how she felt in Tyler's arms. This wasn't her first orgasm or her hundredth, but nothing had prepared her for an experience so moving, so beautiful, so overpowering. No way could she put this into mere words. She didn't even try. She showed Tyler instead.

The water was shallow enough that Kristin could stand and she maneuvered Tyler exactly where she wanted her. She had never done this before, but something felt so natural about her actions that Kristin just knew they were right. She mimicked everything Tyler had done to her minutes ago, her boldness and confidence growing with Tyler's obvious pleasure.

Tyler's breasts were smaller than her own, yet swelled in her palm as she held them. She watched them rise and fall with Tyler's breathing and lowered her head closer to the hard tip. Each breath brought it closer to her lips until she couldn't hold back any longer.

Eagerly Kristin sucked and nibbled on Tyler's nipple and was surprised when it grew harder in her mouth. Had hers done that? Did her body respond to a woman's touch this way? Her need to give Tyler the pleasure she had given her was overwhelming.

Kristin mouthed Tyler's breasts while she let her hands roam her body. Tyler was thin, and any excess fat had burned off during their hardship of the last few days. Her skin was amazingly soft, her curves tantalizing like a treasure map. She cupped the roundness of her ass, amazed how it fit perfectly in her palm. She ran her hand down the back of Tyler's leg and froze when Tyler clenched her wrist.

Through the fog of desire Kristin realized she was touching the amputated leg. Several more inches and she would find nothing left to caress. She didn't care. It didn't matter if Tyler had one leg, no legs, or three legs. She was crazy abut this woman and didn't know what she would do if Tyler didn't let her have her.

Releasing Tyler's breast, Kristin lifted her head. This time fear and apprehension filled Tyler's eyes. Kristin was confused. Certainly a woman as sensuous as Tyler had other women. Was something about her or her technique turning Tyler off? She didn't think so. Tyler wanted her. At least her body did.

Kristin didn't say anything and didn't move as she realized Tyler was uncertain how she would react to her leg. She was afraid it would repulse Kristin, that she would be morbidly curious about making love with a one-legged woman and she would be the topic of conversation over a game of bridge. Kristin's heart hurt for Tyler, for what she must go through every time she made love—if she made love.

Kristin did the only thing she knew—continue gazing into Tyler's piercing eyes until Tyler saw the answer she was searching for.

❖

Stop. Stop right now and you won't get hurt, Tyler repeated to herself. But her body wasn't listening to what her mind was saying. Maybe she couldn't hear it over the hammering of her heart or the roar of her pulse pounding in her head. Maybe she couldn't hear it because for the first time since the accident, she didn't want to.

But she had to listen. Her mind always overruled and her body dutifully went along. She had never let anyone get nearly this close since the accident. The woman in her arms was usually naked, but she never disrobed below the waist. That's what they made zippers for, wasn't it? No one had any clue she had less than what God gave her.

But this time was different. This time she wanted to feel a woman's arms around her, holding her, caressing her, not just fucking her. Her body had always been satisfied but she wanted more with Kristin. She wanted Kristin to touch her.

Tyler was caught in the depths of Kristin's unwavering eyes, as if Kristin were reading her mind, gazing into her soul, waiting for her to make her decision.

Time practically stopped. Tyler was aware only of the exquisite feel of Kristin in her arms. No science, no psychology. Just a sixth sense that she was supposed to be here and Kristin was the woman she was supposed to be with. Tyler teetered on the edge of the unknown. Before she had a chance to talk herself out of it, she jumped.

Releasing Kristin's wrist, Tyler wrapped her arms around Kristin's neck and kissed her. She fought the need to ravage her lips, her mouth, and allow herself to be swallowed by Kristin. She couldn't get close enough when Kristin's hand moved up and down her leg, lingering on the curve of her hip.

Kristin pulled her closer, and with it, her leg rose, sliding her clit higher on Kristin's thigh. Tyler moved against it, and when Kristin locked her mouth around her nipple, Tyler arched her back and moaned.

"Oh, God," Tyler managed to say between clenched teeth. The sensation of Kristin nipping on her nipple instantly traveled directly to the center of her clit with no stops in between. Tyler didn't know whether to close her eyes and dissolve in ecstasy or watch what Kristin was doing to her. She compromised, wanting to memorize every detail of Kristin.

Kristin shifted slightly and her hand slid tentatively between Tyler's legs. Tyler pushed down on her fingers and felt them twitch under her.

"Tell me what to do," Kristin said quietly.

Anything, everything, just don't stop, Tyler wanted to say, and at the look on Kristin's face told her she did. She was on the verge of orgasm right now and didn't want it to slip away.

Tyler tried to kiss Kristin, but she pulled away slightly. Instead she locked her eyes on Tyler as her hand and fingers started to move, more deliberately this time.

Tyler was mesmerized. Kristin was playing her body like she knew every note by memory. Tyler's body was singing, her mind reeling, and she had nowhere to go but with it. She was trapped in Kristin's arms, her back against the slick, cool wall behind the waterfall.

The familiar staccato pulse started in her clit; it would be a matter of seconds before she exploded. She wanted this to last forever, yet wanted to release in Kristin's safe arms. The pounding intensified and every nerve end came alive. She felt every inch of Kristin's naked body pressed against hers, felt their breathing match in and out as they struggled to take a breath. When Kristin whispered in her ear she stopped fighting.

"Come for me, Tyler, please."

The spasms rocked Tyler with such force she was momentarily stunned. Never had her body shook, her breathing stopped, and stars flashed behind her eyelids like this. She was dizzy, the world off its axis. It was the sensation sappy romance books were made of. And she was right in the middle of one.

Wave after wave slammed into Tyler as a multitude of sensations washed through her. She was hot, then cold, weak then strong, all within mere seconds. Or was it minutes? Tyler had no idea how long her orgasm lasted, just that she didn't know if she was more afraid it would end than it wouldn't.

Blackness swam around Tyler and she felt like a voyeur on this scene. She could see Kristin holding her, placing light kisses on her face. She was weightless, floating in air. She hadn't felt like this in, she couldn't remember how long, if ever. This was more than release, it was a convergence of two.

They were cocooned from the outside world and Tyler wanted to stay here forever. Far from the prying eyes, her responsibilities, the world.

"Well," Kristin said, her breathing slowing down. "That was… ugh…nice."

"Nice?" Tyler finally asked, the rockets in her head quieting. She felt Kristin smile against her hair.

"Okay, really nice?"

Before Tyler had a chance to reply another voice drifted into her consciousness. There it was again, louder and clearer. It wasn't coming from Kristin's luscious, magical mouth but from over her shoulder.

"Tyler. You in there? I hope you didn't drown, cause if you did we're in deep shit here."

Paul. She was hearing Paul's voice. Slowly she opened her eyes and blinked a few times to clear the cobwebs of passion that threatened to pull her back in. She wasn't dreaming. She was in Kristin's arms, the water cascading around them forming a secluded cocoon from prying eyes. Like Paul's.

"Tyler?" Paul shouted again. "I see your clothes and—"

Tyler immediately knew Paul had seen Kristin's clothes scattered along the edge of the pond. She looked at Kristin, whose face held the same knowledge.

"Tyler?" This time a question was mixed with the concern.

Kristin started to pull away but Tyler held her still. She put her index finger over her own lips, signaling for Kristin to remain silent.

"Paul," Tyler replied. "Are you alone?"

"Yes, for the moment. Everybody's looking for you and Kristin. Steven's afraid wild animals carried her off."

Tyler almost laughed. Their sex certainly had been wild and animalistic, not that she'd tell anyone.

"I'm fine, Paul," Tyler said, not referring to the fact that Kristin was behind the waterfall with her, let alone had her fingers on her clit. That thought made the organ twitch which, by Kristin's look of surprise, didn't go unnoticed.

"Do you need any help?"

"No, I'm fine," Tyler repeated. She asked Paul to keep watch for a few minutes until she got out of the water, then turned her attention to Kristin.

"As much as I hate to say this, I think you need to move your hand." Tyler spoke with a hint of amusement. When Kristin started to move it, Tyler gasped and grabbed it. "Carefully," she said reluctantly. One more motion from Kristin's fingers as she tried to extricate them from their nest and Tyler would have another orgasm to cope with. And that would be a bad thing because?

"Sorry," Kristin murmured, looking apologetic.

"I'm not," Tyler said quickly, still holding Kristin's hand.

"I'm not either." Kristin's voice was firm and steady.

"I'll get out first and get rid of Paul."

Kristin looked at Tyler, her eyebrows raised. Tyler felt herself blush at the image her statement aroused. "Then you can get dressed. Paul's right. Someone may come looking for us."

"Too bad," Kristin said, floating backward and giving Tyler enough room to swim out from behind the waterfall.

Tyler wanted to kiss Kristin again, but if she did she wouldn't want to stop, and this wasn't the right time or place. What if it hadn't been Paul who interrupted their little tryst?

❖

"What in the fuck are you doing?" Paul whispered as Tyler hopped out of the water. He offered her a steadying hand as she started to put her clothes on. "And no bullshit this time, Tyler. This is not a good thing."

"I'm not doing anything—"

"I said no bullshit, Tyler."

Tyler hadn't seen Paul angry many times, but this was definitely one of them. She remained calm, knowing that two people angry only got uglier. "As I started to say, I'm not doing anything she didn't want to. If you want to get technical she came to me, not the other way around." Tyler sat on the warm rock and slipped her prosthesis on.

"I do not want the details, Tyler," Paul said, cupping his hands over his ears for a second. "I want you to be careful. God knows what Steven would do if he found out."

The realization of what might have been hit Tyler hard. Her actions, lack of control, or whatever she wanted to call it could very well cost Paul his job. Your best friend and your boss's wife is certainly a career-limiting move.

"I'm sorry, Paul. I wasn't thinking about what this might do to you." Tyler was appalled at her actions. Paul was her best friend, and she would never do anything to jeopardize that friendship. Until twenty minutes ago. God, what *was* she thinking? No woman was worth losing your BFF. She hugged him, trying to convey her remorse.

"I'm not worried about me, Tyler. I can take care of myself. I'm worried about you."

This was a surprise. Paul had always been ultra-conservative when it came to his sexuality in his workplace. If she and Kristin were to be discovered, what would that say about him? Would people conclude that if Tyler was a lesbian, then Paul was gay? Tyler doubted this group could draw those two points together.

"Paul, this is your *job* we're talking about."

Paul turned so only his profile was visible. He looked even more ruggedly handsome with a week's worth of stubble.

"If this disaster has taught me anything, it's that life is too short. I'm tired of the lies and secrecy and half-truths. It's been so long even I'm starting to believe them." Paul ran his hands through his short hair, then turned to look at her. "I'm done."

Tyler took his hands. "Paul, think about what you're saying. You've invested a lot in this company, and you said it yourself, just one more big deal and you'll be on your own. You don't want to mess that up now." And Tyler didn't want to be the cause of that mess either.

"What's the point, Tyler, if I can't be myself? I don't want to talk about this anymore." Paul looked around again before he said, "You'd better get you, or her," Paul pointed to the waterfall, "out of here before some other search party finds you."

"I will," Tyler replied, still chastising herself for her thoughtless behavior. How could she have been so stupid?

❖

Camouflaged behind the waterfall, Kristin watched Paul walk away. She couldn't hear what they were talking about, but obviously

Paul was angry. Of course he knew she was here. Her clothes were strewn along the edge of the pond, and unless Paul was blind he had to have noticed them. She had stripped like a seasoned professional in her quest to have Tyler. Quest? Hell, she'd wanted Tyler and she wasn't going to stop until she had her.

Kristin felt herself blush at the memory of just exactly how she'd had Tyler. And how Tyler had had her. It was incredible. She had never been as aroused and alive. Every inch of her skin had ached for Tyler's touch, and every nerve caught fire when she did. It was more than a physical release. It was a hunger unlike anything she had ever experienced. She couldn't explain it. Words weren't adequate to describe what had happened.

But what had happened? Tyler had responded to her without hesitation. Tyler knew exactly what she was doing and Kristin wanted her to do it again. She knew just where to touch her, when she wanted a soft, caressing stroke and when she needed a firm hand. Tyler anticipated her needs and knew her body like a book she had read cover to cover dozens of times. She was a skilled, attentive lover, and somehow Kristin knew she wouldn't stop until she'd had her fill.

"Kristin?" Tyler's voice penetrated her muddled brain. "Kristin?" she repeated more forcefully.

She managed to reply. "Yes?"

"I think it's a good idea if one or both of us got out of here." Tyler looked around as if anticipating one or more of their fellow castaways would walk up any second.

"You're probably right, I'll go." And just how was she going to get out? Kristin felt far less brave walking out of the water naked than she did coming in. She had just shared one of the most intimate acts a woman could share with another, and she was embarrassed to look Tyler in the eye. How ridiculous was that? Thankfully she didn't need to face Tyler or her fears.

"No, I'll go. I'm dressed."

Tyler hesitated. If Kristin could barely see her, then Tyler could see just as much, or maybe even less. She looked like she was about to say something. Kristin waited for Tyler to decide.

"Are you okay?"

How was she supposed to answer that? Her world had completely come unglued, she had been rocked to a core she didn't know she even had, and she doubted if she would even recognize herself in the mirror. She knew exactly what she was doing when it was happening, now she was scared to death.

"I'm all right. You go ahead."

"Be careful then. I'll see you back at camp."

CHAPTER TWENTY-THREE

It was the longest walk of Kristin's life. The trail that led from their camp to the pond was only about sixty yards, but to her it felt like an eternity. What would she do when she got there? Carry on as if nothing had happened? Like she hadn't just experienced the most life-altering event of her life? It had to be written all over her face or, at the minimum, a neon sign overhead that blinked, "Just had wild sex with a woman under a waterfall."

What would she say to Tyler? Would Tyler act like nothing happened? Would she seek Kristin out for a repeat or a confrontation? Surely she wouldn't say anything to Steven. That would be completely insane. It was all so confusing and surreal it made her head pound.

Kristin barely acknowledged the rough path that passed as their trail. Each step brought her closer to…To what? Back to her empty shell of a life? Back to a man she didn't love anymore and hadn't in years? Back to her destiny, whatever the hell that was.

Stalling as long as she could, Kristin emerged from the trees into the clearing. Paul was stoking the signal fire and Tyler was nowhere in sight. Kristin sighed, grateful she wouldn't have to deal with it— whatever *it* was—right away. She was still too emotionally fragile.

Throughout the remainder of the day Steven demanded her attention and Kristin tended to him on automatic pilot. Some of it was habit, some of it probably some bizarre sense of duty, but mostly she just wasn't up to fighting with him if she didn't.

Tyler didn't venture back into camp until after dark, and by that time Kristin was more than a little worried. More than once she had been tempted to ask Paul where Tyler had gone, but didn't know what she'd say to Tyler if she went and found her. When she did make eye contact with Paul, he gave her a sympathetic, understanding smile.

Now Tyler sat in the sand, her back to the fire. Since her return, Kristin had watched her every move and knew she had eaten little more than a few bites of dinner. Paul had tried unsuccessfully to engage Tyler in conversation, and now she was literally alone.

Kristin watched the reflections of the flames dance across Tyler's back. She remembered the feel of Tyler's skin when she touched it. The hard muscles of her shoulders and across her back that trembled under her exploring fingers.

Tyler was more than physically strong. She had endured a terrible accident and had worked hard to get her life back. She was the brains of their survival; without her they would all be in much worse shape than they were. She was an emotional rock, cared deeply for Paul, and Kristin could not even begin to imagine what must be going through her mind.

"Give her time." Steven and the others had been asleep for at least an hour before Paul sat down beside her. "She's got to figure this out," he said.

"Well, when she does I hope she shares it with me," Kristin said sarcastically. "Because I have no idea what's going on."

"I'm a good listener," Paul said after a few minutes. "At least that's what Tyler tells me."

It was dark but Kristin could hear the smile in Paul's voice. "What else does she tell you?"

"It's more of what she doesn't tell me," he replied seriously.

Kristin knew she shouldn't push. Shouldn't pry into Tyler's life, her privacy like this, but she desperately needed to know what Tyler was thinking so she asked anyway. "Like what?"

Paul hesitated as if he, himself, was deciding just how much to share with her. Kristin wanted to ask again but didn't. She had done enough to these two.

"That she's lonely," Paul said, surprising her. "She buries herself in her writing and tells everyone she's on a writing binge. That the story just has to get out." Paul chuckled. "But that's bullshit and I've told her so. Then she tells me I'm full of shit, and we change the subject and talk about something else."

Kristin nodded her understanding. "I can see that. Admittedly I don't know her that well." Kristin paused and almost burst out laughing. What a ridiculous statement. They had fucked each other senseless. "She seems to really have it together."

"It's an act. She lives her life in the same fiction world as her writing. She doesn't let anyone get too close. Not many people know about the accident. It's as if she thinks that if she doesn't talk about it, it didn't happen. But every step she takes, every move she makes reminds her of that day."

"She told me you were there for her, after the accident," Kristin said, prompting Paul to continue.

"Yeah, Jessica called me from the hospital. At first I thought she knew Tyler wanted me there, but it wasn't long before I realized Jessica wanted to be anywhere other than with Tyler. What a worthless piece of human being she turned out to be."

Kristin was afraid to say anything for fear that Paul would stop talking, and she definitely wanted to hear more, especially about Jessica. Paul must have read her mind.

"She hung around for a few months when it was easy, when all she had to do was visit Tyler in the hospital or rehab center. A few hours here and there and her conscience was clear. But the work really began when Tyler came home."

"Was she her partner?" Kristin asked hesitantly. She didn't know if "partner" was the right word to use. Girlfriend? Lover? Significant other?

"I think Tyler thought so, but Jessica obviously didn't. Tyler was a convenience for Jessica. Someone to go running with, backpacking, biking, you know that sort of thing. Tyler apparently didn't know how much she expected she could depend on Jessica to help her until she didn't. I guess Tyler called her on it one night, Jessica got ugly, and that was that. Tyler's barely said her name since then. If I bring her up I get the I'm-not-going-to-talk-about-this-with-you look. And nothing can change her mind. Believe me, I've tried."

"She's lucky to have you," Kristin said, envious. She had few friends, certainly not one like Paul.

"I'm the lucky one," he replied, almost reverently.

They sat in silence for several minutes before Kristin asked what had been on her mind most of the day. "Why did you tell me where Tyler was this morning?"

"Because she's my best friend and she needs somebody in her life."

Kristin didn't expect that answer at all. "And you think that somebody is me?"

"Yes, I do. She's different with you. I can see it in her eyes, the way she talks about you, the way she talks *to* you. She's told you things she's never told anyone."

"It's just the circumstances. We're fighting for our lives here. That's got to make people do things they normally wouldn't." Even Blake Hudson had said as much in several of her equally bizarre situations.

"Not Tyler. She's the most focused, self-controlled person I know. She doesn't do anything she doesn't think about or doesn't want to. There's just something about you, Kristin, that changes her. I saw it the first moment you two met years ago. She didn't have a clue, but she often doesn't about these things. I know her better than she knows herself."

"Did you ever tell her?"

"No. She wouldn't have heard a thing I had to say. She wasn't ready."

"And you think she's ready now?" Kristin asked, afraid if the answer was yes, and even more afraid if it was no.

Paul nodded in Tyler's direction. "That's why she's been sitting there for the past three hours."

Kristin didn't know what to say. She was stunned, joyous, and scared shitless. But wasn't she in the same position as Tyler? She'd had no idea she would find herself desperately attracted to a woman. To Tyler.

But that wasn't the half of it. She had found herself again. She had been gone so long she hardly recognized herself. She used to be strong, self-reliant, and unafraid. Where had that woman been all these years? How had Kristin let her slip away? She vowed to never let it happen again.

"Paul? Are you gay?" Kristin asked, knowing her question was inappropriate. But nothing about this last week had been appropriate.

"Yes."

Kristin knew how much he had risked by answering her question honestly, and she touched his arm. "I'm sorry." Paul looked at her, clearly alarmed.

"No, I mean I'm sorry you've had to keep this hidden all these years." Paul visibly relaxed. "No one should have to hide who they are just to have a job."

"But I love my job," Paul said, almost defensively.

"I know you do, but you shouldn't have to pretend, especially to work for an ass like Steven." And I never should have let him convince me to quit mine because I was married to him, she thought.

"Well, I don't think I'll have to worry about that when we get off our little patch of paradise,"

"He won't hear it from me," Kristin said quickly.

"No," Paul said confidently. "He'll hear it from me."

CHAPTER TWENTY-FOUR

K ristin! Get over here. Now."
Tyler was returning from catching their breakfast when she heard the anger in Steven's voice. Hell, everyone and everything on the island could hear it. Suddenly Tyler was anxious. Something was up. She heard what sounded like a muffled cry. Tyler hurried down the path.

Upon entering the clearing she saw Kristin standing in front of Steven, her hand over her mouth. He had managed to get to his feet, a large boulder behind him taking most of his weight. Everyone within spitting distance except Paul stood. Their body language conveyed enough tension to blanket the air around them, even if they were in the middle of a deserted island.

Then Tyler noticed blood between Kristin's fingers. It trickled down the back of her hand. Anger flashed through her and she hurried her pace.

"What did she do to you?" Steven hissed. He was directing his anger toward Kristin, still oblivious that Tyler had returned.

"Nothing," Kristin replied, wiping the blood from her hand on the leg of her shorts.

"Don't tell me 'nothing,'" Steven bellowed. "Joan saw you two…down by the water…and you were…" He stammered, his face red with fury.

Tyler's stomach dropped and Kristin immediately went pale. *Oh, fuck.*

"Steven," Kristin said.

Steven raised his hand to backhand Kristin and Tyler stepped closer. "Don't touch her." Even to her own ears, her statement sounded like the threat it was.

Steven stopped and glared at her. "Well, if it isn't little miss I-know-how-to-survive-in-the-wilderness." Steven smirked.

"What's going on?" Tyler risked a glance around, looking for Paul. Where was he? This was going to get ugly in about two minutes.

"I'm talking about the disgusting things you did to my wife."

Okay, less than two minutes.

"Don't deny it." Steven's voice was a snarl. "I have witnesses. You forced yourself on my wife."

Steven's use of the phrase *my wife* three times in a row was clearly meant to assert his claim over Kristin.

"Steven—" Kristin said.

"Shut up," he hissed, spittle practically dripping off his chin. His face and neck were beet red, and not due to the sun. He looked like he was about to explode.

"Steven," Paul said, finally appearing from out of nowhere.

"You stay out of it," he snarled. He pointed at Paul. "If you were more of a man…had more control over *her*," Steven pointed his chubby finger at Tyler, "this wouldn't have happened."

"Now it's your turn to shut the fuck up," Tyler said, her jaws clenched. She was exercising all her self-control not to deck the fat man in front of her. He was always disrespectful to Kristin, and now he turned his ugliness on Paul. Two strikes against him.

"Is that the way you talk when you and Pauly-boy have sex? I'll bet you tell him exactly what to do. I bet he has to have Viagra to get it up with you."

Tyler was drawing back her fist when Paul started to laugh. His belly laugh only came when something struck him as completely hilarious. She dared a glance at him, not sure if he thought this entire scene was hysterical or he was hysterical.

"Don't you get it, Tyler?" Paul asked between gasps. "Stevie-boy is right," he said, mimicking the childish name. "I would need

Viagra to get it up with you. Maybe even two or three." He took a deep breath, then added, "What a waste of a good pharmaceutical."

Tyler didn't join Paul's laughter but maintained her focus on Steven and Kristin. She had no idea what Steven would do in this situation and wanted to be prepared for anything. Kristin, however, had shifted and now stood beside her, her shoulders straight, her head held high.

"What the fuck is going on?" Steven demanded, looking at the three of them. He obviously sensed something was not as it appeared.

Tyler looked at Paul for confirmation and he nodded his support.

"The joke is on you, Steven," Paul said. "She's not my girlfriend."

Steven still hadn't gotten Paul's meaning. She had said earlier that some people wouldn't know a lesbian if they were kissing right in front of them. People like Steven would find it arousing even if he thought it disgusting.

"I'm a lesbian, Steven."

Tyler watched her words sink into his bigoted brain. As they did, his face turned red and angry again.

Tyler couldn't help but laugh along with Paul this time. "You just don't get it, do you, Steven? It wouldn't matter what Paul did or didn't do. I'm still a lesbian."

Steven swung his attention from Paul to Tyler and back again. "Then that makes you—"

"That makes him *my* best friend." Tyler had interrupted Steven before he could spew out another of his ugly tirades. "And because he *is* my best friend I'm willing to put up with shit like this for him." Tyler used her hands to indicate their surroundings. "Paul is like any other single, red-blooded adult male. He dates and I'm sure he even has sex, without medical enhancements," she added for effect. "He just hasn't found anyone he wants to settle down with, and until he does he calls me when society, namely *you,* demands he bring a guest. Would you rather he *hire* someone?"

"You're a dyke and you're trying to turn my wife into one."

Tyler hoped she'd diverted his attention from Paul. She had to convince him that whatever Joan said she had seen, she was lying.

"For God's sake, Steven, you don't make people gay or lesbian. You either are or not. It's in your DNA," Kristin said from beside her.

Tyler looked at Kristin, surprised. During the last few days Tyler had noticed a shift in Kristin's interaction with Steven. She no longer jumped when he called, and on more than one occasion she had talked back to him. No longer was Kristin the dutiful wife standing behind her man. She was now standing in front of him, and not just literally.

"But she's after you," he said, pointing to Tyler.

"No, she isn't," Kristin replied calmly. "I'm a grown woman, Steven, and even if you don't think so, I am perfectly capable of making my own decisions. No one makes me do anything I don't want to. Not anymore," she added firmly.

"Everybody knows she's going to try to turn every woman she sees into one of them," Steven told Kristin, his voice full of hate and disgust.

Tyler had to speak up. "Steven, you're so full of shit I don't understand how you get through the day. I'm attracted to women who are attracted to women. Straight women don't interest me. I can appreciate the beauty of a woman—her brains, her character, her strength—but unlike men, that doesn't mean I want to have sex with them. I'm a lesbian, I don't seduce straight women. I don't have to. When I make love to a woman it's because she wants me as much as I want her. As for the women on this island," Tyler intentionally didn't mention Kristin, "I have no more interest in touching them than I do their husbands."

Tyler turned to their audience. The men were quiet, the women gaping. "So you can all go back into your safe little world and tell all your friends at the club that you met a real, live lesbian."

Paul chose that moment to jump out of the closet and into the light of day. "Since we're setting the record straight here—no pun intended—I'm gay, Steven. Complete, one hundred percent gay. Always have been, always will be, and if you don't like it, too bad."

Given the circumstances, Tyler felt pretty good about herself and was very proud of Paul. Her best friend was by her side, their charade was over. Tyler held her breath, not knowing what to expect from Steven but prepared for anything.

"I'm not through with you," Steven said.

Tyler turned and saw he was talking to Kristin. She started to come to her defense again when something in Kristin's eyes stopped her. Something she had never seen before.

"Fuck you, Steven," Kristin said calmly.

Steven was obviously stunned but quickly recovered.

"Don't you dare talk to me like that," he growled through clenched teeth. He tried to move closer to her, but Kristin stepped forward instead.

Kristin felt stronger than she had in years and invaded Steven's personal space until she was practically nose to nose with him.

"Or what?" Kristin was surprisingly calm and at peace for the first time in she couldn't remember how long. She refused to take his shit anymore.

Other than the waves crashing in the distance, there was complete silence. Kristin knew everyone was looking at her but waiting for Steven's reaction. She didn't care. What was he going to do other than what he'd done more times than she could remember? No, that wasn't right. She had *let him* more times than she should have. But that was stopping, right now.

"Or what, Steven?" Kristin knew she was taunting him but couldn't stop. "What are you going to do? Fire me? Don't bother. I quit."

"Kristin, this is not the place—"

"This is exactly the place. Actually, any place will do. It was okay for you to talk to me the way you did in front of other people, but it's not okay for me to do the same? Don't you think that's a bit of a double standard?" Kristin took advantage of one of the few times he was silent. "I'm done, Steven. Done with your arrogance, your attitude, and your bullshit. What I ever saw in you I'll never know because what I see now disgusts me."

Steven was almost purple with rage and Kristin expected him to keel over with a stroke any second. She started to walk away but stopped and turned to the stunned faces, but addressed her comment to Steven. "Oh, and you know all about the little blue pill, don't you, Steven?"

Kristin took Tyler's hand and pulled her toward the privacy of the trees.

CHAPTER TWENTY-FIVE

Tyler stumbled over the rough ground and Kristin stopped, allowing Tyler to catch her breath. Kristin had been practically in a sprint since leaving the scene on the beach.

"Are you okay?" Kristin asked. Her expression mirrored the concern in her voice.

"I'm fine." Tyler's leg hurt, but what else was new? "Where are we going?"

Kristin looked around as if seeing their surroundings for the first time. Tyler could tell she was still angry. "Any place that isn't near them," she answered, using her thumb to point over her shoulder. "What a fucking circus."

Tyler couldn't help but smile at her word choice.

"What's so funny? Please share it with me because I lost my sense of humor years ago. And my self-respect."

"It's just that I suspect you've said the word *fuck* more in the last five minutes than you have in five years. This probably isn't the right thing to say, but it suits you."

"It *suits* me?"

"Yeah." Kristin still held her hand and it felt good. "I don't know how to explain it. It just rolls off your tongue, sharp and to the point. It's very effective." Tyler also thought it was sexy, but this wasn't the right time to go there.

Kristin finally relaxed and returned her smile. "It felt good too. I should have said it years ago. God, what a wuss I turned into."

Kristin dropped her hand and sat down on a dead tree stump. Tyler sat close beside her.

"What happened to me? One day I was a young, self-confident woman charting my course through life, the next someone who couldn't say shit if I had a mouthful. God, I'm disgusting." Kristin dropped her head into her hands.

"I wouldn't call what you did back there being a wuss. It was pretty ballsy."

Kristin's laugh filled the air and Tyler's stomach jumped into her throat. The sound was like music. "Now it's my turn to ask what's so funny."

Kristin was still laughing when she looked at her, her face alive, her eyes clear and bright.

"That's a pretty good play on words. Ballsy? We're talking about lesbians and seduction and sex, and you call me ballsy. No pun intended, I hope?"

The sheer joy now radiating from Kristin made Tyler breathless. It had hurt to see her berating herself, but this? She wanted to see it forever.

That thought stunned her. Forever? Where did that come from? She didn't want forever. Hell, since the accident she hadn't wanted anything more than right now—and pretty superficially at that.

Images of Kristin in her kitchen in San Francisco making dinner, fussing over a salad or grilling on the patio, flashed through her head like a parade. The next frames pictured Kristin sitting at Tyler's table paying bills or surfing the Web. They switched to her on a lounge chair on the patio enjoying a glass of wine as the sun set over the bay, then to sitting quietly in the large wingback chair in her office as she banged out Blake's latest adventure on her laptop. Then she was lying in bed waiting for Kristin. Holy Christ. What was all this about?

Tyler realized Kristin was waiting for her to speak. What had she said? Was she was supposed to answer a question? She had absolutely no clue and must have looked confused.

"Tyler?" Kristin touched her arm.

Sparks of desire shot through Tyler where Kristin was touching her. She wanted Kristin right here, right now, in the light of day. She wanted to see her naked, feel the sun warm her bare skin. She wanted absolutely nothing between them but passion, desire, and the sweet sweat generated from their bodies. She had never wanted anyone as much as she wanted Kristin, and certainly not as openly.

Tyler's world rocked in that moment and she froze with the implications. Kristin had seen her, all of her, and had not been repulsed. Kristin had seen her struggle over the past week and was always there, willing to help because it was the right thing to do, not out of pity or obligation.

But she couldn't do this. Not with Kristin. Kristin had found herself again on this island, and she didn't intend to put similar strings around her. Kristin needed to live her life the way she wanted to, and at this point she probably didn't have the slightest idea what that was. She was not going to stand in her way.

"I'm sorry, what did you say?" Tyler pulled herself together, which wasn't easy.

"You look a little peaked?" Kristin touched her cheek as if checking for a fever. Tyler jerked back and Kristin quickly dropped her hand.

"Sorry," Tyler said quickly, to erase the hurt on Kristin's face. "I'm fine. Just…I'm…I think we should go back," Tyler finally managed to say.

"Go back?" Kristin sounded as if Tyler had asked her to jump off a cliff. "I'm not going back."

Tyler couldn't think straight with Kristin touching her so she stood to break the contact. "Kristin, this isn't the time or situation to be making major decisions. This isn't reality."

"And what do you define as reality?"

"What you see and do everyday. What you have to do to eat, have a roof over your head and clean clothes. It's stability and being safe."

"Well, reality isn't all it's cracked up to be. I would know."

"Kristin—"

"Don't Kristin me. You sound condescending and I've had enough of that."

Kristin's words cut through Tyler like a knife, and she choked back a sob. "That's not what I meant."

"Then what do you mean?"

Tyler had no idea. Nonsense was spewing from her mouth. She was a talented, award-winning, best-selling author, for crying out loud. A conveyor of words into stories that people disappeared into. And here she was unable to string two thoughts together.

"This is a pretty big deal, Kristin. Deciding to leave Steven. You need to think about the ramifications."

"I already know the ramifications. I don't love him, haven't loved him in years. I don't like the person I became during our marriage, how I let him dominate me and my life. It took this trip, this crash..." Kristin stood and took Tyler's hands. "It took you to get me to see all that."

"Don't," Tyler said. She couldn't be the reason or the solution.

"Don't tell me what to do or not do. I will not let you or anyone else tell me what I should or shouldn't do, or feel or say, for that matter. My emotions are real, and whether you like them or not, that's what they are. I'm not backing down. Not anymore."

The fire in Kristin's eyes, the attitude her body conveyed, her strength made Tyler fall completely in love with her. Head-over-heels, breathtaking, heart-stopping love. But she had to let Kristin go. She had to let her continue her journey, wherever it led her.

"I'm sorry. I didn't mean to imply anything. We've all changed this week. And if this is what you want, I'm happy for you." She *was* happy for her. Didn't you always want the woman you love to be happy?

Kristin couldn't read Tyler's expressions fast enough. They shifted from joy to fear, confusion, and desire practically with each statement. Regardless of what Tyler said, Kristin was sure about what she wanted. Her marriage to Steven was over, had been over for years. All that was left were the technicalities. She would deal with the fallout and support her parents, get a second job if she had to, but she could not stay married to Steven any longer.

And she wanted Tyler. Wanted to be in her life, share her life with her. They had already shared many of the ingredients of a relationship—*the better and for worse* and *in sickness and in health* part. The *love, honor, and cherish* phase was just beginning, and she wanted the *as long as ye both shall live*. And she wanted it with Tyler. All she had to do was convince her.

She let go of Tyler's hands and cupped her face. Her skin was soft and several shades darker than when they'd stepped on the plane a week ago. Her mouth more tempting than she ever realized. Kristin looked deep into Tyler's eyes searching for a sign, any sign that Tyler might feel the same. That she might want to try to build something together. Then Kristin realized that even though she might not be able to see it right now, she knew a way she could tell. She kissed her. Tyler's body, her touch wouldn't lie.

Tyler was tentative at first but Kristin didn't give up. She had to make Tyler understand how much she wanted her. This wasn't just physical need. Kristin wanted to feed off Tyler's strength, learn from her, be everything to her. She wanted to support Tyler when she needed it as well. She nibbled on Tyler's lower lip and lightly ran her tongue over the outline of the top one. She teased Tyler's mouth open and left her gasping for breath. Kristin pulled Tyler closer, their breasts moving against each other as Tyler's breathing became shallow and fast.

Tyler finally responded, wrapping herself around Kristin, pulling them even closer. Kristin dragged her lips from Tyler's mouth and trailed hot, wet kisses up and down her neck at the same time she slipped her hands under Tyler's shirt. Tyler gasped at her light touch yet her breasts swelled in her palms. "Kristin," she whispered.

That was it! What she was waiting for. Tyler had been through a lot. She'd been hurt and had physical limitations that deeply affected her. She was operating in full self-protection mode. It made perfect sense. She might not be ready to say the words, but her touch, her kiss, the way she responded to her touch told Kristin everything she needed to know.

CHAPTER TWENTY-SIX

Tyler pulled Kristin to the ground, faintly remembering that anyone could walk up with little warning, but she doubted anyone would. The foliage was rather thick, and someone would have to practically fall over them. She didn't care. She was tired of fighting her attraction to Kristin, hiding her self-doubts about her body. With Kristin it didn't matter. Nothing mattered except being with her.

Tyler wanted to go slow, savor every moment and memorize every inch of flesh exposed by zippers and buttons. She knew that every time with Kristin would be like the first time. Every quiver, shudder, tremble of her limbs would be like fuel to her parched soul. This is what she wanted. But Kristin had other ideas.

"Take your clothes off," she breathed into Tyler's mouth, pulling her shirt out of her shorts. "Hurry."

Kristin's enthusiasm and obvious arousal was like a strong aphrodisiac. She sat up and pulled her shirt the rest of the way over her head. Her nipples hardened even more when Kristin licked her lips.

Tyler pulled Kristin to a sitting position and practically tore the buttons from the thread. She dispensed with Kristin's bra and laid her own shirt on the ground to protect Kristin's back from the leaves and small twigs.

"No, let me," Tyler said, stopping Kristin from unzipping her own shorts. Their eyes met, Kristin's blazing with desire matching her own. In two quick movements Kristin's shorts and panties were off. Kristin's long, firm legs fell open and Tyler could only stare and marvel at her beauty. Kristin's arousal was evident as she glistened in the early morning sun.

Kristin was the most beautiful woman she had ever seen. Her skin was soft, with the requisite lines and curves, peaks and valleys, and Tyler wanted to explore it from the bottom of her feet to the tip of her nose. She wanted to trace her freckles with her tongue, tickle the back of her knees with feather-light kisses, and eat strawberries off the hollow spot on her stomach. Words like *gorgeous*, *exquisite*, and *magnificent* came to mind but didn't even begin to describe what Tyler felt.

"In case I wasn't clear, you *may* look *and* touch," Kristin said playfully. "Let me rephrase that. You had *better* look and touch. And you'd better do it soon before I do it myself."

The low throbbing between her legs intensified and Tyler was swept away with the need to do anything to please Kristin. It was more than a desire, it was pure, raw need. She needed Kristin like she'd never needed anything in her life. She needed to feel her touch, see her response, breathe her air. Somehow Tyler found her voice as she lowered her body onto Kristin's.

"As much as I'd like that, and God knows just how much I would, we'll save that for later, much later."

Kristin pushed her away, tugging Tyler's undershirt. "Oh, no, you don't. I want all those clothes off. Every thread. I want to see you clearly this time, not have your body blurred by the water. *All of you.*" Out of habit Tyler hesitated, and Kristin kissed her hard then looked her in the eyes.

"I don't care. It doesn't matter. I need you, Tyler. All of you," she repeated.

The sincerity in Kristin's voice and the honesty in her eyes erased any lingering doubts. Tyler sat up and pulled off the remainder of her clothes. Her hands shook as she unhooked her prosthesis for the first time in front of a woman. She knelt before Kristin feeling scared and safe in the same instant. She swallowed hard as Kristin's eyes traveled over her body, lingering on her breasts and between her legs. She held her breath when Kristin frowned at the scars on her stomach and where her left leg once was.

Tyler was ready to bolt when Kristin spoke, a catch in her voice. "You are beautiful. Absolutely beautiful." She reached for her hand and pulled Tyler down. "Please make love to me, Tyler. I can't wait any longer."

Time and reality ceased. Tyler moved her hands across soft skin, down long, hard legs and into silky warmth. She teased and licked and sucked Kristin's breasts, giving equal attention to each hard nipple. Tyler barely felt Kristin dig her fingernails into her back. Kristin was so responsive in her arms, Tyler was overcome with emotion.

Kristin moaned in pleasure when Tyler lightly bit one nipple. Kristin grabbed Tyler's hair, holding her mouth close as she raised her leg and wrapped it tight around her thigh. When Kristin whispered her name it was the sweetest sound Tyler had ever heard.

Tyler lifted her head from Kristin's breasts and smiled when Kristin pulled her back. "I have to taste you," Tyler said, tracing the outline of a nipple with the point of her tongue. "You feel so good against me and on my fingers. I have to have you."

Kristin let go of her hair and Tyler shifted her weight, then covered Kristin's stomach with kisses. Tyler stroked and teased the soft, sensitive skin between Kristin's legs. She traced the outer edges, moving closer to her clitoris with each stroke. Kristin lifted her hips in the universal signal of desire, and Tyler couldn't deny either of them any longer. Lightly she flicked the hard bud and was rewarded when Kristin stiffened and inhaled sharply.

Tyler froze, thinking she had hurt or frightened her. She had done this same thing in their coupling under the waterfall, but this entire setting was different. That was sex. This, out in the open, completely exposed, was very, very different. It felt more powerful and intense than what they had shared in the water. Kristin had every right to be frightened. Tyler was scared to death.

"Don't stop," Kristin begged her, clearing up any doubt in Tyler's mind. As Tyler moved closer to what they both wanted, she slid her finger into Kristin's opening. Kristin lifted her hips again and shuddered. Tyler thought Kristin had climaxed.

"Put your mouth on me, Tyler, please. I need your mouth, your tongue." Kristin's legs were bending up and down as she spoke.

Tyler's world completely shifted. She had never wanted a woman like she wanted Kristin. Wanted to pleasure her, give her everything she wanted and needed. At this very moment she existed solely for Kristin's pleasure. She didn't intend to disappoint her.

Kristin smelled wonderful. Tyler would never forget her musky scent and her first taste of her. She used her tongue to explore the inner recess of the woman who had captured her heart. She flicked her tongue across Kristin's clit, used the flat surface to bathe her with deep, firm strokes, all the while moving first one then two fingers in and out of her.

Tyler fought to keep up with Kristin's rapidly increasing movements. Her hips rose higher, giving Tyler complete access. Tyler wanted to watch Kristin come, wanted to see her face fill with pleasure as orgasm overtook her. Lifting her head just a fraction, what she saw took her breath away.

Kristin's back was arched, her legs splayed wide, and Kristin was pinching her own nipples. But what stopped Tyler's heart was that Kristin was leaning on her elbows looking right at her. She was watching everything Tyler was doing to her.

"Don't stop, please, Tyler." Her words were a cross between begging, pleading, and demanding. Tyler burned this moment into her brain for eternity.

Kristin stiffened an instant before her orgasm. She came before Tyler was ready, preferring to continue exactly what she was doing for hours, if not days. Kristin's orgasm was strong, and Tyler wasn't sure where one ended and another began. She also wasn't sure when her own orgasm started, their bodies so in tune.

Kristin thought she would faint. Her head pounded, stars flashed behind her eyes, and she couldn't breathe. Every nerve was on overload, and she prayed this didn't kill her and would last forever. She had never had an orgasm this powerful and intense. Mechanically it was the same. But her lover was absolutely everything. Kristin couldn't imagine being with anyone other than Tyler, who had captured her heart and released her body. This was completely right.

Catching her breath she opened her eyes. Tyler was gazing at her from her position between her legs, and she looked scared. Was Tyler afraid she would bolt, after what had just happened? But then Kristin realized tears were running down her own cheeks. Tyler's touch had brought her to tears.

"Tyler—" She heard shouting on the beach they had just left. She couldn't make out anything, but everyone sounded excited.

Tyler heard them too and was scrambling into her clothes. Kristin followed, and as she buttoned her shirt a loud roar came from overhead. She looked up just in time to see an orange-and-white helicopter skim the treetops.

CHAPTER TWENTY-SEVEN

Tyler hadn't boarded the coast-guard helicopter yet. She didn't want to be the first evacuated, and given the pushing and shoving of some of her more selfish castaways, she didn't have to insist.

She and Kristin hadn't had a chance to say anything to each other since their rescuers arrived. They had dressed quickly and hurried back to the camp just as the helicopter was landing. The men in orange jumpsuits and bright white helmets spilled out of the open cargo door, and Tyler experienced an overwhelming wave of relief. They unloaded bottles of fresh water and food and started checking out each survivor.

Even with one crewmember staying behind, the helicopter could hold only four, and forty-five minutes after they landed, Joan and Patty were strapped into their seats, along with Steven and his newly splinted leg. Kristin had refused to accompany him.

"Kristin," Steven hollered. "Get in here with me where you belong."

"No. I'm not going anywhere with you, Steven. I meant what I said. You're on your own."

"Kristin, I'm warning you. Get in this helicopter."

"Get it through your thick head, Steven. I'm not going with you."

"What are you going to do then?" The pain medication the crewman had given Steven obviously hadn't dampened his nasty streak.

"I'm staying with Tyler," Kristin said, looking directly at her. "If she'll have me."

Tyler's heart jumped. She wanted Kristin to stay, wanted to disappear back into the wilderness together and never come out. But she was scared. Hell, she wasn't just scared, she was scared to death.

"You, in the red shirt, get on board," the coast-guard lieutenant said to Robert. He turned his attention to Tyler and Kristin. "You two figure it out by the time we get back. We don't have all day to get you all out of here." It would take at least ninety minutes for the helicopter to reach land and the same to return for the second load. In total, it would probably take several hours to evacuate everyone. He slid the door shut and the rotors started turning. Paul and Mark turned their back on the blowing sand and walked back to the camp to wait.

When the helicopter was little more than a disappearing speck in the sky, Kristin spoke.

"Tyler?" Kristin laid her hand on her forearm. The same jolt of energy she always felt when Kristin touched her multiplied tenfold. Her legs started to tremble and she sat down on a large rock. Kristin spoke again. "When you told Steven you had no interest in straight women, did that include me?"

It did, but it certainly didn't now. What a cluster fuck her heart had gotten her into. "Yes," Tyler lied.

"Then how do you explain what happened? It sure seemed to me you wanted to." Kristin stood to her left, hands on her hips in a very defiant pose. She was strong and proud, and Tyler's heart cracked a little more.

"I can't," Tyler said, completely defeated. "I can't explain it other than to say I'm sorry that I upset you and I never want to do that again."

"What?" Kristin asked. When Tyler didn't immediately answer, Kristin took her chin and forced her to face her.

"Look at me."

Tyler couldn't bring herself to see the pain in Kristin's eyes.

"I said look at me, Tyler," Kristin repeated.

This time she obeyed.

"You think I'm upset? What made you think that?"

Tyler didn't answer.

"Answer me, Tyler."

"You were crying," Tyler managed to say. She didn't want to have this conversation. She didn't want to experience the pain she felt when she saw Kristin's tears. She tried to use anger to mask the pain.

"I made you cry. I did those things to you…made you cry. It doesn't take a mathematician to put two and two together and figure out what the answer is."

"For someone who kept us alive for more than a week, you're pretty clueless about some things."

"Kristin, this is all really new to you. This," Tyler said, palms up indicating their surroundings, "this isn't the real world. You need to get back to your home, back into your normal life, then make your decisions." God, it hurt to say that. She really wanted to say, Yes, I do want you. I want you today, the day after that, and ten thousand tomorrows. But she didn't. Tyler looked down at her shaking hands. She was about to completely fall apart. She had never felt like this and never wanted to again.

"Time isn't going to change my mind, Tyler. I'll go back into that house only to get my things, and I'm not so sure I even want anything. As for my normal life…" Kristin chuckled. "My normal life begins now. I want you in that life, Tyler. I want to spend the rest of my life convincing you of that." She took a deep breath. "But if you don't want that, tell me now. As much as I may want to, I refuse to beg. I'll never allow myself to be put in that position again."

Tyler wanted to say yes. She was tired of being alone. Tired of fighting to keep her fears at bay, of facing life with one leg alone. She wanted to share her success with someone she could bounce ideas off, someone to help her pick names for her characters and critique her work. Someone to make her life story come alive.

"I have one leg," Tyler said out of the blue.

"I'm partially deaf in one ear." Kristin countered her.

"I get so wrapped up in my writing I don't come out of my office for days."

"I can't ride a bike."

"I have a small apartment."

"I'll have an ex-husband."

"I have a best friend I'd do anything for."

"I want a dog."

"Blake is a lesbian."

"Duh!"

"My editor is very possessive."

"I love you."

"I get cranky under deadline."

"I love you."

"I'm not much of a risk taker."

"I'll catch you."

"My brother will tease you."

"I love you."

"I call my leg Lucy."

Kristin laughed at that one. "I love you."

Tyler jumped off the cliff with both feet. "I love you too."

"I think I can live with that."

"I know I can." Tyler pulled Kristin into her arms and kissed her.

The End

About the Author

Julie Cannon is a corporate stiff by day and dreamer by night. She has eight other books published by Bold Strokes Books: *Breaker's Passion, Descent, Power Play, Just Business, Uncharted Passage, Heartland, Heart to Heart,* and *Come and Get Me.* Julie has also published five short stories in Bold Strokes anthologies. A recent transplant to Houston, Julie and her partner Laura live on the lake with their two kids, two dogs and a cat.

Books Available From Bold Strokes Books

High Impact by Kim Baldwin. Thrill seeker Emery Lawson and Adventure Outfitter Pasha Dunn learn you can never truly appreciate what's important and what you're capable of until faced with a sudden and stark reminder of your own mortality. (978-1-60282-580-2)

Snowbound by Cari Hunter. "The policewoman got shot and she's bleeding everywhere. Get someone here in one hour or I'm going to put her out of her misery." It's an ultimatum that will forever change the lives of police officer Sam Lucas and Dr. Kate Myles. (978-1-60282-581-9)

Rescue Me by Julie Cannon. Tyler Logan reluctantly agrees to pose as the girlfriend of her in-the-closet gay BFF at his company's annual retreat, but she didn't count on falling for Kristin, the boss's wife. (978-1-60282-582-6)

Murder in the Irish Channel by Greg Herren. Chanse MacLeod investigates the disappearance of a female activist fighting the Archdiocese of New Orleans and a powerful real estate syndicate. (978-1-60282-584-0)

Franky Gets Real by Mel Bossa. A four day getaway. Five childhood friends. Five shattering confessions…and a forgotten love unearthed. (978-1-60282-585-7)

Riding the Rails: Locomotive Lust and Carnal Cabooses edited by Jerry Wheeler. Some of the hottest writers of gay erotica spin tales of Riding the Rails. (978-1-60282-586-4)

Sheltering Dunes by Radclyffe. The seventh in the award-winning Provincetown Tales. The pasts, presents, and futures of three women collide in a single moment that will alter all their lives forever. (978-1-60282-573-4)

Holy Rollers by Rob Byrnes. Partners in life and crime, Grant Lambert and Chase LaMarca assemble a team of gay and lesbian criminals to steal millions from a right-wing mega-church, but the gang's plans are complicated by an "ex-gay" conference, the FBI, and a corrupt reverend with his own plans for the cash. (978-1-60282-578-9)

History's Passion: Stories of Sex Before Stonewall, edited by Richard Labonté. Four acclaimed erotic authors re-imagine the past…Welcome to the hidden queer history of men loving men not so very long—and centuries—ago. (978-1-60282-576-5)

Lucky Loser by Yolanda Wallace. Top tennis pros Sinjin Smythe and Laure Fortescue reach Wimbledon desperate to claim tennis's crown jewel, but will their feelings for each other get in the way? (978-1-60282-575-8)

Mystery of The Tempest: A Fisher Key Adventure by Sam Cameron. Twin brothers Denny and Steven Anderson love helping people and fighting crime alongside their sheriff dad on sun-drenched Fisher Key, Florida, but Denny doesn't dare tell anyone he's gay, and Steven has secrets of his own to keep. (978-1-60282-579-6)

Better Off Red: Vampire Sorority Sisters Book 1 by Rebekah Weatherspoon. Every sorority has its secrets, and college freshman Ginger Carmichael soon discovers that her pledge is more than a bond of sisterhood—it's a lifelong pact to serve six bloodthirsty demons with a lot more than nutritional needs. (978-1-60282-574-1)

Detours by Jeffrey Ricker. Joel Patterson is heading to Maine for his mother's funeral, and his high school friend Lincoln has invited himself along on the ride—and into Joel's bed—but when the ghost of Joel's mother joins the trip, the route is likely to be anything but straight. (978-1-60282-577-2)

Three Days by L.T. Marie. In a town like Vegas where anything can happen, Shawn and Dakota find that the stakes are love at all costs, and it's a gamble neither can afford to lose. (978-1-60282-569-7)

Swimming to Chicago by David-Matthew Barnes. As the lives of the adults around them unravel, high school students Alex and Robby form an unbreakable bond, vowing to do anything to stay together—even if it means leaving everything behind. (978-1-60282-572-7)

Hostage Moon by AJ Quinn. Hunter Roswell thought she had left her past behind, until a serial killer begins stalking her. Can FBI profiler Sara Wilder help her find her connection to the killer before he strikes on blood moon? (978-1-60282-568-0)

Erotica Exotica: Tales of Sex, Magic, and the Supernatural, edited by Richard Labonté. Today's top gay erotica authors offer sexual thrills and perverse arousal, spooky chills, and magical orgasms in these stories exploring arcane mystery, supernatural seduction, and sex that haunts in a manner both weird and wondrous. (978-1-60282-570-3)

Blue by Russ Gregory. Matt and Thatcher find themselves in the crosshairs of a psychotic killer stalking gay men in the streets of Austin, and only a 103-year-old nursing home resident holds the key to solving the murders—but can she give up her secrets in time to save them? (978-1-60282-571-0)

Balance of Forces: Toujours Ici by Ali Vali. Immortal Kendal Richoux's life began during the reign of Egypt's only female pharaoh, and history has taught her the dangers of getting too close to anyone who hasn't harnessed the power of time, but as she prepares for the most important battle of her long life, can she resist her attraction to Piper Marmande? (978-1-60282-567-3)

Wings: Subversive Gay Angel Erotica, edited by Todd Gregory. A collection of powerfully written tales of passion and desire centered on the aching beauty of angels. (978-1-60282-565-9)

Contemporary Gay Romances by Felice Picano. These works of short fiction from legendary novelist and memoirist Felice Picano are as different from any standard "romances" as you can get, but they will linger in the mind and memory. (978-1-60282-639-7)

Pirate's Fortune: Supreme Constellations Book Four by Gun Brooke. Set against the backdrop of war, captured mercenary Weiss Kyakh is persuaded to work undercover with bio-android Madisyn Pimm, which foils her plans to escape, but kindles unexpected love. (978-1-60282-563-5)

Sex and Skateboards by Ashley Bartlett. Sex and skateboards and surfing on the California coast. What more could anyone want? Alden McKenna thinks that's all she needs, until she meets Weston Duvall. (978-1-60282-562-8)

Waiting in the Wings by Melissa Brayden. Jenna has spent her whole life training for the stage, but the one thing she didn't prepare for was Adrienne. Is she ready to sacrifice what she's worked so hard for in exchange for a shot at something much deeper? (978-1-60282-561-1)

Suite Nineteen by Mel Bossa. Psychic Ben Lebeau moves into Shilts Manor, where he meets seductive Lennox Van Kemp and his clan of Métis—guardians of a spiritual conspiracy dating back to Christ. But are Ben's psychic abilities strong enough to save him? (978-1-60282-564-2)

Speaking Out: LGBTQ Youth Stand Up, edited by Steve Berman. Inspiring stories written for and about LGBTQ teens of overcoming adversity (against intolerance and homophobia) and experiencing life after "coming out." (978-1-60282-566-6)

Forbidden Passions by MJ Williamz. Passion burns hotter when it's forbidden, and the fire between Katie Prentiss and Corrine Staples in antebellum Louisiana is raging out of control. (978-1-60282-641-0)

Harmony by Karis Walsh. When Brook Stanton meets a beautiful musician who threatens the security of her conventional, predetermined future, will she take a chance on finding the harmony only love creates? (978-1-60282-237-5)